KILLER PINE

by the same author

COLD WAR IN A COUNTRY GARDEN

LINDSAY GUTTERIDGE

KILLER
PINE

Jonathan Cape Thirty Bedford Square London

FIRST PUBLISHED 1973
© 1973 BY LINDSAY GUTTERIDGE

JONATHAN CAPE LTD, 30 BEDFORD SQUARE, LONDON WCI

ISBN 0 224 00829 3

PRINTED IN GREAT BRITAIN BY
EBENEZER BAYLIS & SON LTD
THE TRINITY PRESS, WORCESTER, AND LONDON
ON PAPER SUPPLIED BY P. F. BINGHAM LTD
BOUND BY G. & J. KITCAT LTD, LONDON

To Marjorie and to Jane

LODGEPOLE PINE (Pinus Contorta)

Grows in Western North America, from Alaska to California, both along the coast and on inland mountain ranges. Called *Lodgepole* because Indians used its straight stems to support their lodges and wigwams. Its bark breaks into small, thin, squarish plates, divided by shallow furrows. The timber is like that of the Scots Pine and has similar uses. Lodgepole Pines have great tolerance of poor soils. (H.M.S.O. Forestry Commission Booklet No. 15.)

PART ONE

One

The red ant was in a savage mood. It ran this way and that, its shining, ruby-red, armoured body the only bright spot in the gloom.

A small rise in the afternoon temperature had roused its dormant instinct to leave the nest and hunt for food. Now the cold evening air urged it to rejoin the mass of comatose insects huddled in underground galleries.

The small insects that were its natural prey were still hibernating or buried in their pupal state, yet its instinct to return with food for the colony drove it on through the forest of Brussels sprout stalks.

This war between opposing instincts – to return home or continue hunting – set its nerves on edge. It jerked its head restlessly to and fro, clashed its jaws, and was about to turn back towards the distant nest when it heard a noise from the lower slopes of the allotment. It backed into the shadow of a sprout stalk and waited.

A line of rooks flew across the allotment. Below them the land turned grey and black in the fading light. Water-filled footprints between the rows of stripped Brussels sprouts reflected the cold winter sky; it was a desolate landscape like a miniature battlefield, the footprints like craters and the plants like shattered trees.

Eleven micro-men came hurrying between the

towering plants, eager to get home before the light went.*

The ant came out of ambush like a rhino charging a line of porters. The men scattered. It was savaging a fallen man when the platoon leader shot it from behind. The crossbow bolt struck a leg, the beast fell, then scrambled up and escaped across country, trailing the crippled limb through the mud. Afraid that it might bring back others if it went free, the leader went in pursuit; but in spite of its injury the ant outran him. The micro-man knelt, aimed quickly, and hit it squarely in the hindquarters. Spurts of vapour shot out of the breathing tubes along its sides and it collapsed and disappeared. Its pursuer found it half-submerged in a water-filled hole, its armour streaked with yellow clay, a film creeping over the six hundred lenses of each great compound eye.

The squad leader returned, pushed through the group and knelt by the injured man. There was blood on the man's sleeve and the leader slit it open to examine the arm. He splinted the arm with a cross-bow, securing it with draw-strings from the hood and waist of an anorak, then the two biggest micro-men linked arms to make a chair and the party trudged on up the hill.

They came over the rise and saw before them the cliff face of a garden shed. Hurrying down the slope they came out on the footpath, climbed the threshold and passed beneath the enormous door. The leader lingered on the threshold; he heard a hoarse croak from above and he looked up and watched a straggler flapping like a wet, black rag towards the uproar in a

* A micro-man stands below the description of the Lodgepole Pine on page 7.

distant rookery. The air was full of moisture and the smell of rotted leaves; he watched the mist drifting down the slope, then turned abruptly and walked into the shed.

At first only a point of yellow light was visible in the dark, then as his eyes adjusted to the dimness he saw the bench, shelves, garden tools and the pile of sacks in a corner. His men marched down the shed towards an old wooden box in the middle of the floor. Dim light lit its grey façade, revealing a cracked and flaking pattern of veneers. It towered a foot above the approaching men and high up, near the top, a rectangle glowed.

The injured man now walked with the help of his comrades and the leader overtook his platoon as they came to the base of the box; he struck the wall with the butt of his crossbow, a door opened and he stood aside and counted them in.

'Get Roberts to the doctor, Sergeant.'

'Yes, sir. Do you want a report?'

'No. I'll see him in the morning. Good night, Sergeant.'

'Good night, Captain Dilke.'

The men walked from the vestibule into the glare of light in the box interior and the officer stepped into an open-fronted lift and pressed the single button in the cage wall. The lift rose rapidly.

He stepped from it into his flat, stripped off his wet clothes and showered noisily and energetically, then entered the main room wearing a towelling robe, rubbing hard at his thinning hair.

He was a man nearing forty; a big, muscular, thick-waisted micro-man a quarter of an inch tall, quick and deft in his movements like a pro wrestler. From his broad, flat face jutted a thin scimitar of a nose, adding a touch of nervous arrogance to his features.

Built in the lid of the box, the room resembled an architect's conversion of an old mill. The huge bars and springs and brass walls of the original lock-chamber had been retained. The furnishings were modern. In place of the original lock facia and key-hole was a glass wall with a sliding section opening on to a balcony; through it light shone out into the vast garden shed. Across the room from the balcony window an observation window gave a view into the box interior.

Two framed pictures hung on one wall: a da Vinci sketch of a Swiss archer setting a crossbow and a photograph of a Milanese bow in a museum showcase. Between them hung a primitive crossbow with a worn stock carved from wood, its bow and bowstring made from insect cartilege and spun filament. In striking contrast, a dozen insect heads were mounted on the facing wall like trophies in a hunting lodge – ants, wasps, cicadas, centipedes, a fruit fly ... arranged symmetrically around the grotesque head of an ant lion with a quarter-inch horn span.

Kneeling at a coffee table covered with papers, her head bent over a typewriter, was a young Negress wearing black slacks and a voluminous grey sweater.

'You've brought the office home, then,' he greeted her.

'It was so cold down there, and I thought *you'd* soon be home.'

He sat on the sofa behind her and leaned forward to touch the nape of her neck with his lips.

'What sort of day?' she murmured.

14

'Bloody wet! Bloody cold!' he said, 'Bloody England!'

She twisted round and sat propped against the low table.

'You want your sweater!'

'No. Scotch will do.'

He wandered across to the window overlooking the great hall and thoughtfully watched two men at target practice.

She came to him with a full glass balanced on the tips of the long fingers of one hand, offered ceremoniously but mockingly. He took the glass and pulled her to him, feeling her thin body through the heavy folds of the sweater.

When she left him to tidy away her papers he remained, drinking whisky, resting his forehead against the window, his eyes following the two men on the floor below. He had a hundred men in training already and there was room for many more.

He felt some satisfaction with the progress they had made. Though there were deficiencies in the organization, it was early days yet ... they could be rectified.

It was a good set-up, he thought. The box as a base; then the rough shelter of the shed for them to learn the first facts of micro-life; then the world of the allotment.

But was it all too easy?

The men he was training had been spared the traumatic sufferings of the few micro-pioneers who had preceded them—were they any better for that? Dilke was not impressed by the reactions of the patrol to the ant's attack.

He recalled his own brutal introduction to micro-life;

thrown naked and without shelter into a terrifying new dimension, alone and unarmed against the monstrous dangers of an insect-dominated world ...

Dilke had a flash of self doubt. He looked round at the new rugs and furnishings of the room.

Was he turning soft himself?

This had been his first micro-home; it had been a dank metal chamber with a keyhole for an entrance and a massive brass cover as a sliding door, attainable only after a near 300-millimetre climb up the outside of the box.

Now he had a lift. Dilke smiled wryly. Progress!

'I have some messages from head office,' the girl called.

Mathew Dilke grunted.

'Major Price rang.'

He turned his head. 'What did *he* want?'

She stood by the table turning the pages of her notepad. 'One: your book on survival is now on the stocks, how many copies will you want? And two: he wants to speak to you about a mission which he wouldn't discuss with me.' She flipped the spiral-bound pad shut. 'Why doesn't he like me?'

'He's a misogynistic bastard.'

'He doesn't approve of us!' She waited for a response. '*Does* he?'

'It's none of his business, Hyacinthe.'

He left the window to refill his glass, then crossed to the girl on the sofa. He stretched out with his head in her lap and nested the glass in the hair on his chest ... 'Forget Price, my sweet. I'll ring him tomorrow.'

At nine-thirty Hyacinthe rang Whitehall from the flat:

'Captain Dilke for Major Price.'

He took the phone and gazed through the balcony window into the winter-dark morning of the shed interior and waited.

'Good morning, Major Price, Dilke here. Miss Kasama tells me the book is ready for printing. I think two hundred copies will be enough for a first impression. I hope to have a lot more information for a second edition.

'Will you please arrange to have the book's charts and illustrations put on slide so that I can project them for the men here? And I suggest that a few full-size copies are printed so that future volunteers can read it before being miniaturized ... '

The voice on the line interrupted him; then Dilke continued ' ... I realize that reading the book may put some men off, but that might be a good thing, Major. I'm not running a rest-home.

'Miss Kasama also says that you spoke of a mission. What is it about?'

The voice buzzed a reply.

'Can't you tell me what it is *now*? Is it espionage?' asked Dilke.

The buzz rose a semitone.

Dilke echoed the reply ' "Something for Lord Raglen ... " but you can't say what?'

The voice buzzed irascibly.

'This may not be a good time for me to leave the training camp, Major Price.'

Major Price's voice sounded a little shrill to Hyacinthe.

'All right, Major. I'll appoint a deputy and I'll ring you later today about a pick-up date.' Dilke replaced the phone and snorted: 'He wouldn't tell you what

the mission is because he doesn't know himself!'
He rose and walked to the door. 'I'm going to see
John Settle. See you over at the office.'

Dilke stepped from the lift on to the floor of the hall
and paused by the class on orientation.

Sixty men were grouped in front of an outsize
aerial photograph of the shed and the allotment.

An instructor was drilling the men on local geo-
graphy. 'You must adapt to a new scale. Remember,
you are reduced to about one-quarter of an inch tall —
one three-hundredth of your normal size.'

He turned to a blackboard and chalked, $\frac{1}{300}$.

'This photograph shows an allotment one hundred
feet long but to you it will appear three hundred times
bigger — more like six miles long. A gardener in it will
seem to be a third of a mile high and he will seem to
walk at nine hundred miles an hour.

'Coincidentally, one millimetre is almost exactly
three-hundredth of one foot.' He turned and chalked
on the board, ONE MILLIMETRE = ONE FOOT.

'Remember this simple equation. If you remember
that each millimetre now seems like a *foot* to you, you
will soon adjust to your new scale of things. I am six
millimetres tall; this hall is three hundred millimetres
long; the garden shed is two and a half thousand
millimetres high — like half a mile high to you ... '

Dilke moved on to eavesdrop on the marksmanship
class. They were studying dead insects at the side of
the shooting range; the body of a hunting wasp had
been sliced down the centre and suspended on a cable
from the roof of the hall for the purpose of displaying
vulnerable parts.

Dilke asked one of the men listening to the cross-bow instructor if he had seen John Settle.

'Over on the mat, sir, I think.'

In a corner of the hall nine men in judo outfits knelt round a wide, circular mat. A black-belt with J. SETTLE stitched in neat letters on the hem of his tunic was demonstrating a spectacular sequence of throws and locks on a sweating novice.

As Dilke approached, Settle released the white-belt and came to the edge of the mat. 'Carry on with your breakfalls, gentlemen,' he called to the class, and: 'You wanted me, Captain Dilke?'

'Yes I do, let's have coffee.'

They left the sound of breakfalls behind and entered the main block.

A man with his right arm strapped across his chest sat alone in the canteen. The table was littered with empty cups; he paused in his moody stirring of a fifth coffee to give Dilke a pale smile.

'You O.K., Roberts?'

'Yes, sir. Just a cracked collarbone and a few cuts.'

Dilke nodded and crossed to a seat by the window, and Settle poured coffees at the deserted canteen bar and brought them over.

'I have to go to Whitehall and I need a deputy here in my absence.' Dilke sipped his coffee and squinted through the window into the glare of the light in the hall. 'I don't know how long I'll be gone. How do you feel about taking over?'

'When will you be leaving, Captain Dilke?'

'As soon as possible.'

Settle gazed at his distant class hurling itself into the air and falling *en masse*.

'I have a fair idea of how the centre runs but I'm short on detailed knowledge – apart from that I'd be glad to take over.'

'Good. A couple of days in the office with Miss Kasama – who will be going with me by the way – will tell you all you need to know. I'll speak to the section leaders before I go – will you fix a meeting please?'

They pushed canteen tables together to make a committee table and Dilke told them that he was leaving them for a time and putting Settle in charge. Then he raised a thick folder of papers from the table. 'I've checked the progress notes I've kept since your training started; you get top marks for weaponry, communications and orienteering – but show not the remotest idea of what your training is really about. You are technique obsessed, gentlemen.'

He dropped the folder to the table.

'You are here to *survive* – not just to attend lectures!'

He looked grimly at the silent men.

'You are now *micro-men*. This is not just the world you knew made small. Outside this base is the insect world. And there you must face the biggest, fastest, strongest, nastiest enemies you've ever met. Some of your men have not even been into the garden shed. You can't put it off – get fit! get hard! and get out into the field.'

Dilke paused. There were no comments.

'From tomorrow a new system will operate. A

round-the-clock guard will be kept on all approaches to the shed. Each unit will take turns and two men from each unit will spend a week on the shed roof, there's a way up the honeysuckle on the west wall and there's shelter on the roof under its leaves. It will seem like a half-mile climb ... ' Dilke smiled grimly ' ... and they'll damn near freeze up there!'

The men scraped back their chairs, shifted the tables and filed silently from the canteen. As Dilke rose to leave he caught John Settle's eye. 'There is a time for shock treatment,' he grinned.

By ten on Friday morning Dilke and Hyacinthe had bathed, breakfasted, dressed and laid out their kits.

At eleven a call came through from the guard posted in the shed window; a man had driven up in an old Rover and was walking down the allotment path.

They finished their coffees and climbed a shaft leading to the roof of the box. Dilke pushed up the hinged cover and they crawled on to the box top. They stood and faced the shed door, a key turned in the padlock and the door scraped open along the worn furrow in the wooden floor.

A huge silhouette almost filled the doorway.

Dilke experienced the sensations of disbelief and apprehension which he always felt in the presence of a man of normal stature.

A twelve-volt battery wrapped in polythene was on the threshold. The man paused, stooped to pick it up then swayed into the shed, leaning back from its weight. He dumped the battery beside the one which supplied the box with power. The impact bounced the box off the floor. Hyacinthe screamed and clutched at Dilke and they fell forward on hands and knees. 'Great clumsy bastard!' Dilke growled. He scrambled up and glared at the huge crouching figure transferring the power leads from the old battery to the new.

The man loomed over the box; his searching eyes blinked, diminished by the thick lenses of his glasses; the fog of his breath enveloped them. He took a metal object the size of a cricket ball from a pocket and put it on the box lid, then lumbered out of the shed with the old battery.

They walked through the mist to the shining ball and went up a ramp into its interior; the flywheel of a huge gyroscope almost filled the sphere and its central column rose from floor to ceiling.

They dropped their bows, quivers and bedrolls on the couch which encircled the carpeted floor. Dilke pulled a lever on the control panel and the gyroscope began to spin; the growling of the central column on its bearing changed to a deep hum; he watched the flywheel blur into top speed.

He left the container and stood beneath its curve, looking out through the open shed door.

Outside, the courier languidly pulled up Brussels sprout stalks and dropped them on the compost heap. When he'd pulled up a dozen plants he rubbed his fingertips together, dabbled them in the water-butt and dried them on his handkerchief. He glanced at his watch, lit a Senior Service and leaned in the shed doorway. He was a portly man in a ginger suede coat with a grubby lambswool collar and a brown corduroy hat; more like a sports commentator than a civil servant, thought Dilke.

The man smoked the cigarette down to a fifteen millimetre stub and lobbed it into the sprouts patch; as he stepped through the door Dilke re-entered the transporter.

Two

In spite of the stabilizing effect of the gyroscope it was a turbulent journey.

Dilke and Hyacinthe followed their progress by the lurches and bumps; the sudden pick-up and pocketing of the container; the thud on to the dashboard shelf; the bumping ride over the allotment road; the stop, go, stop of London traffic after the long motorway drive; the swing into the Whitehall car park and the final crash on to a ministry desk.

Early in the journey they were thrown off the couch and had remained on the carpeted floor. Dilke now picked himself up and left the chamber.

The transporter was grounded on a blotting-pad which lay on a big, leather-topped desk.

Dilke paused at the foot of the ramp and remembered his first visit to the room. Eighteen months ago, at midnight, he had stood with two companions in the middle of a snow-white blotter, lit by the blinding glare from a desk lamp. Lord Raglen had peered through a lens at them as if they were insects before giving them a peremptory briefing. Dilke had been awed by the immensity of Raglen's body and provoked by his arrogant manner.

Now Dilke stepped off the ramp dizzy with motion sickness and Hyacinthe followed him across the yielding surface of the blotting-paper towards the centre of the pad.

Cold light flooded into the high room through floor-to-ceiling windows which were framed by faded velvet curtains. A boardroom table, protected by a felt cover, stood beneath a huge, crystal chandelier. Two antique electric fires supplemented the heat from a glowing coal fire and from above the wide mantelshelf Joseph Chamberlain — in oils — gazed sombrely down the long room.

A plump man in a morning suit stood at a distant window with his back to the room. He was sipping coffee and looking through the circle he had cleared on the steamed-up glass. A fold of flesh rolled over his high collar as he tilted his head to drink; the movement revealed a strand of hair adhering to the polished dome of his head. Then he left his peep-hole on to St James's Park and walked towards the desk.

In Dilke's eyes he grew in stature at each great step until he stood, a colossus, between desk and chair.

Lord Raglen took a last sip and put down the cup beside the blotting-pad; he took spectacles from his breast pocket, put them on and stared down at the silver sphere. Then he glanced sharply over the half-moon glasses: 'Thank you, Bellamy.'

The dismissed courier left the room and the great chandelier jangled softly in the current of air from the closing door.

Lord Raglen sat down. The extended fingers of the vast hands came together to form a steeple, the point of which lay beneath his lordship's nose. From behind semi-circular lenses his pouched eyes searched the surface of the blotter.

To make detection easier Dilke stepped forward three paces and swung his arms above his head. A smile moved the great cheeks and Raglen parted his hands in an abbreviated arc of acknowledgment.

'I am pleased to see you again, Captain Dilke. I believe your micro-training programme is going well. Well enough to permit your absence for a while, Price informs me. It'll do your men good; make them stand on their own feet!'

Raglen's giant hand passed overhead, lifted the wooden lid of a canister as big as a gasometer and abstracted a cigar.

'At any rate, I have a job for you of more immediate importance than putting trainee micro-men through the mill.'

Two massive fingers dipped into a waistcoat pocket and withdrew a gigantic silver-plated cigar cutter. A fleshy white hand cut a notch in the cigar end with ponderous adroitness and the huge wedge of Cuban tobacco crashed down into a cut-glass ashtray. A banner of flame gushed from a matchhead.

'The Canadian forests are dying, Captain Dilke.' Raglen paused as if for dramatic effect. 'They have some sort of blight, I'm told, and I'm sending you out there to investigate. Before I hand you back to Bellamy I want to stress the importance of this mission.

'The blight started in Canada but has now spread down through the States as far as New Mexico.

'The governments of Canada and America take this business very seriously and if it gets out of hand it could affect the U.K. too. Timber is a most important industrial raw material. Without it many industries would suffer – even the plastics industry uses it.

'The problem has already been thoroughly researched. You may find nothing. It's a long shot. Bellamy will get you anything you want: equipment, specialist advice and so forth, and he will take you out there.'

Lord Raglen stretched out and pressed a button on the intercom. 'Send in Bellamy, Miss Graveney.'

The moonface smiled down upon the minute figures.

'Goodbye, Captain Dilke. And good luck!'

Dilke and Hyacinthe turned and walked away towards the sphere. The discarded matchstick – only partially extinguished – had rekindled and set fire to the tobacco in the ashtray. Flames leapt within the cut-glass walls and a haze of smoke drifted across the blotting-pad. They ran, and entered the sphere with stinging eyes; in a little while they felt a surge of movement as the transporter was lifted from the desk.

The information room which Bellamy shared with two other intelligence officers and an indoor plant with pink flowers and fleshy stalks, was furnished with sludge-green metal furniture and Dexion racks holding books of reference and stacks of the world's newspapers.

Bellamy had placed the transporter on his desk. Dilke and Hyacinthe sat on a paper-clip under the curve of the sphere and watched him. Throughout the afternoon Bellamy did routine work until his colleagues cleared their desks and locked up their files at five-thirty.

'Are you staying on, Mr B.?' the woman called.

'For a little while, Miss Davis; you can leave the keys with me.'

'We've seen to the windows and I've watered the Busy Lizzie.' They said their good-nights and dropped the keys on his desk on their way out. When they had gone he locked the office door and reseated himself. He gave three deliberate taps with his fingernails on the desk top as an invitation to Dilke to show himself and Dilke moved out from the shadow of the transporter.

The great eyes focused upon him.

'Captain Dilke. My name is Gilbert Bellamy. I am to take you to Canada and Lord Raglen has asked me to brief you on the trip. I'm sorry to have kept you waiting but ... ' the suggestion of a smile shadowed the corner of his mouth ' ... I didn't want the department to think I was talking to myself.' He reached into a desk drawer and placed a matchbox reverently before him.

'Before I start I think we should make contact. In here', he rested a finger on the matchbox, 'you will find a telephone hook-up through which you can talk to me.' Bellamy twisted his head and squinted at the box. 'There is a door in the side somewhere.'

They crossed the desk and inspected the box. It was a convincing fake, made of steel with 'Brymay Matches — British made' printed on one side and a purple striker stuck on the other. The end wall was a sheet of clear perspex. A sliding door in the box side gave access to a vestibule: a narrow observation chamber with a row of body-contoured seats which faced the window. They passed through into the inner chamber of the transporter. It had cupboards and a refrigerator, a radio transmitter and an electric clock. There was accommodation for twelve, with a row of two-tier bunks along a wall and a big table fixed to the floor. Metal conduits carried power from a concealed battery to the electrical equipment.

The effect was Spartan; rather like a naval wardroom
– though the composition flooring was soft underfoot.
The place smelled like a new car.

The case containing the telephone hook-up had
slipped off the table and spilled a heap of cable on to
the floor. While Hyacinthe disentangled it Dilke
read the instructions. It was a line-tapping device, a
miniature of the sort used by G.P.O. repair engineers,
enabling Dilke to talk to Bellamy when it was wired
to his telephone.

They repacked the equipment in its case and
carried it out of the matchbox.

The office was now dark; Bellamy's great phone was
spotlit by the desk lamp; they looked up at his looming
figure crouched watchfully over the desk, and then
carried the case towards the high ebony wall of the
distant telephone. There was enough space beneath
the instrument for them to walk under it and a row
of ventilation holes in its base gave access to its
interior.

'Jump up, Hyacinthe, and I'll pass the gear to you.'
He made a stirrup for her foot with his hands, then
handed her the case and finally climbed up himself.
It was dark inside the phone and it took them a while
to locate the hook-up terminals, even with light from
an electric torch. At last they found them high on a
junction panel; Hyacinthe held the torch and Dilke
climbed with the double-headed cable. The phone's
terminals were thick with grease to which wads of
fluff had stuck. He pulled off the fluff, scraped two
areas of metal bare, then attached the magnetic
heads which clunked satisfactorily into place. He
plugged in the sound booster and they left the telephone interior, paying out the cable behind them as

they went. Dilke walked a dozen paces from the telephone and stared up at Bellamy who now lay back in his chair with the telephone receiver caught between his neck and shoulder, the earpiece against an ear, the mouthpiece pressed into the flesh beneath his chin.

The miniature receiver in Dilke's hand was of an unconventional design; attached to one end was a dialling cylinder, Dilke wondered if he must dial Bellamy's number – but only the rim of the big phone's chrome dial was visible and he could not see its exchange number.

He put his lips to the mouthpiece and spoke slowly and distinctly: 'Testing. One, two, three. Testing. One, two three,' and he watched the face.

Bellamy slowly raised a huge forefinger in salute, 'Good evening, Captain Dilke, how nice to hear you. And good evening, Miss Kasama, I hope your new quarters are comfortable.'

Hyacinthe smiled with pleasure.

'Now for the briefing, Captain. How much has Lord Raglen told you?'

'He gave me an outline of the mission's purpose, Mr Bellamy, and said how important it is.'

'The Canadians and Americans *do* seem to be in a flap,' Bellamy agreed.

For a moment he gazed down upon the two tiny humans then he laid the telephone receiver on his desk.

'I'll begin at the beginning.' He rose heavily and brought two rolled charts from a shelf and hung them on a wall near his desk. The top chart showed the North American continent, from the Pole to the Panama Canal. It had been marked with a dozen red crosses, scattered in a random way down the long line of the Rocky Mountains.

'During the last four years there have been outbreaks of a mysterious tree disease on the North American continent,' Bellamy began.

'Its appearance has followed no discernible pattern but it is spreading faster and faster and the foresters have been unable to check it. As yet it has damaged only a small percentage of forest land but the alarming thing is that the cause of the disease is not yet known. The disease's *effects*, however, are well understood. Trees are like fountains of water. A big tree sucks up tons of water a day through its roots – a liquid solution of nitrogen and mineral salts on which it lives. The water travels up a network of tubes in the trunk and branches, then passes out through pores in the leaves as a vapour. The leaves regulate the flow by opening and closing their pores. The infection paralyses the leaves so that the pores remain open and water flushes out ceaselessly carrying with it the minerals without which the tree cannot live.'

Bellamy looked moodily at the map. 'In a way, the tree bleeds to death.

'This is where the trouble began.' His spread hand covered about four hundred miles of Canadian Rockies. 'The first infestation started in British Columbia up near the Yukon border. The following year it broke out again a few hundred miles south (and simultaneously in other places) and a year later it started here in the mountain foothills.' Bellamy tapped the map, 'And this is where I am taking you, Captain Dilke.'

He removed the top chart to reveal a close-up of the area of devastation. Someone had marked a cross on a high ridge then drawn a series of concentric circles around the mark.

Dilke and Hyacinthe walked out of the shadow of the phone to get a better view.

'This is a record which the Canadian Forestry Manager has kept since the outbreak started two years ago. The circles were drawn at three-monthly intervals and they indicate the spread of the disease – as you see, the bands are getting narrower, showing that the rate of spread is now slowing down . . .'

Bellamy hesitated and looked at his watch. 'But these details are on micro-file, Captain Dilke, and you can study them before we leave England. I expect that's enough for one day ... unless you have any questions?' He raised the telephone to his ear.

'Thank you, Mr Bellamy. No questions – you have made things very clear. Before you go will you move the matchbox nearer to your phone so that I can take my extension into it – and please leave a light on.'

Bellamy nodded and smiled. He moved the match-box, deposited the office keys in a wall safe then put on his coat and left.

They took a walk on the desk before going indoors. The distant bulb threw long shadows from the desk calendar and filing trays. They strolled together round the desk's perimeter and looked down upon a sea of linoleum. In half an hour they had made the circuit; the matchbox was hidden in the shadow of the telephone but a slit of light from its half-open door revealed its position. They entered and prepared a meal, then as they sat at the table after supper Dilke idly picked up the phone and dialled a number. He listened with a smile and passed the receiver to the girl.

Hyacinthe laughed and they recited in unison: '...at the third stroke it will be nine, forty-two, and twenty seconds Precisely!'

They went to their beds early.

Though Dilke and Bellamy could speak together through the desk phone during office hours the erratic behaviour of the line puzzled the switchboard —and the talks had to be initiated by Bellamy as Dilke could not ring him up.

Dilke asked to be moved to a place from which he could dial Bellamy at the information office.

Bellamy took them to his home—a flat in a flaking Victorian terrace which overlooked the Thames— and placed the matchbox beside a telephone on a window-ledge.

The new arrangement worked well; they could talk together at the flat in the evening and during the day Dilke could phone the office.

He listed the things they needed for the trip: cameras and film and writing materials; outdoor clothing, a stock of concentrated food and camping gear.

Dilke studied the file of information on the tree disease. It was written by botanists for botanists and its language finally defeated him. 'Jargon!' Dilke threw it aside irritably and phoned Bellamy. 'I will need a specialist on tree diseases. There is no one back at the training depot who will do, have you anyone at headquarters?'

Bellamy discovered that an ecologist was halfway

through his miniaturization at Westminster Hospital.

The man's name was Jonathan Butt. Though he was not a specialist on trees he had a broad knowledge of plant life – 'it may be *better* for him to have peripheral knowledge, Captain; he might see things a specialist would miss.'

Butt's miniaturization was to be completed in a few weeks.

Bellamy was allowed into the security wing of the hospital, and was taken by a white-coated physician to Butt's bedside. He casually put down the Brymay box on the bedside cabinet and Dilke and Hyacinthe leaned forward in their seats to stare at the childlike figure lying with closed eyes under the white sheet, lit by the evening light which filtered through slatted blinds.

The physician sat on the bed and its occupant opened his eyes; eyes which were dark against the pallor of his face, the pupils excessively dilated, black circles with narrow brown irises.

'Good evening, Jon,' smiled the doctor. He stretched out a hand and clicked on the bed-head light. His patient shut his eyes. He took a compliant wrist, lightly rested his fingertips on the pulse and gazed at his watch. The silence in the room seemed complete. The soft, fast tick of the watch gradually asserted itself and the folds of the starched, white coat creaked to the rhythm of the doctor's breathing.

He released the wrist and scribbled a reading on the chart.

He took a flat case from his pocket and from it took a hypodermic syringe and a small glass ampule. He snapped off the brittle head of the phial and carefully filled the hypodermic. Raising the needle to eye level, he slowly depressed the plunger: a thin jet of colour-less liquid shot up and fell in a curve to the floor.

He pushed back his patient's loose sleeve and swabbed his forearm. A chain of needle marks followed a vein up the arm. Nine small craters, each with its flushed bruise; purple to green to fading yellow.

'Soon the process will accelerate; it should be complete in three weeks.'

He made the tenth injection low on the forearm, withdrew the needle and swabbed the wound.

'That is your last jab. We are halfway through the treatment, but from tonight I'm switching you to pills.'

He produced a small brown jar, took from it a capsule and presented it for inspection between finger and thumb. The case of the capsule was transparent, revealing dozens of miniature yellow capsules. 'Big fleas have little fleas upon their backs to bite 'em and little fleas have smaller fleas and so on ad infinitum,' he quoted sententiously. 'The little capsules contain even smaller ones. As time passes I will phase out the drugs – and the graded sizes of the capsules will make this easy.'

He leaned forward and put the capsule on the white top of the bedside locker. 'Take this after supper.'

...ked at his watch, checked the pulse beat and ... a second reading on the chart.

...will sleep a lot from now. These second stage ...ve hallucinatory side effects and I've added a ... to give you some rest. In case you become ...wsy to understand me later, I want to say a ...out diet: when the treatment is finished you will be thirsty – drink little and often; take lots of protein but keep off sugar.'

He stood up and smiled. 'Good night, Jon.'

The wan face did not smile, but the head nodded.

Three

Watching Bellamy in the rather threadbare comfort of his flat, seeing him eat and drink and perform his bachelor chores, reduced the formality of their relationship. Soon they were using Christian names and sometimes watched television together and listened to records. Bellamy liked a good tune and had a taste for the Edwardians; he was a D'Oyly Carte man.

Less than a fortnight after their arrival at Bellamy's flat, he turned up one evening looking smug. 'I have a surprise for you, Mathew.'

Producing the gyro-transporter he placed it on the window ledge, then drew up a chair to watch.

Dilke passed the smiling face and the huge pebble glasses which almost touched the ledge, and entered the silver sphere. The gyro was still running and Dilke crossed to the control panel and switched it off. The chamber seemed empty, but when he walked round the central column he found a seated man, a man almost as tall as himself, extraordinarily broad and extremely emaciated—whose eyes were sunk in cavernous sockets and whose hollow cheeks were shadowed by a stubble of beard.

He nodded a slow acknowledgment to Dilke's greeting.

'Jonathan Butt?'

'Yes.'

The man rose heavily and Dilke shook the extended hand; a big, bony hand with rough, dry skin.

'I'm Mathew Dilke and I'm glad to meet you. You seem to be ahead of schedule.'

'I am.'

Dilke looked with curiosity at the man, who had an unmistakably Scottish accent despite his English name. Butt had nothing with him except the clothes which hung on his gaunt frame; they left the transporter, passed the watching Bellamy and entered Brymay.

Hyacinthe greeted the new arrival awkwardly, surprised at his strange appearance – and the presence of a Negress seemed to puzzle the man.

Dilke left them, took the phone extension outside and grimly signalled to the waiting Bellamy.

Bellamy lifted his receiver and Dilke snapped, 'They've sent me a *sick* man!'

Bellamy's smile faded. 'But they say the labs have passed him O.K.'

'They've rushed his treatment. Who's been pushing them?'

Bellamy gave a delicate shrug.

'Has Raglen been breathing down their necks?'

Bellamy remained silent.

'It's a farce!'

'I'm sorry, Mathew.'

'It's not your fault, Gilbert. But this is absurd. They've pushed this man's treatment through at the risk of his health.' Dilke took a deep breath. 'Anyway, it'll do no good, it will be weeks before he'll be fit!'

Dilke turned away and strode into the box. Bellamy watched him wryly, then slowly lowered the receiver into its cradle.

Hyacinthe had prepared supper and Butt silently awaited Dilke's return. When they were seated their guest drank three glasses of water in succession.

'Drink little and often,' Dilke gently reminded him.

'They've dried me out.' Jonathan Butt wiped his mouth dourly, and then ate a prodigious meal.

Dilke discovered that Butt had been a short, stocky man – no more than five feet four inches – and that the premature ending of his miniaturization had given him the equivalent height of a tall micro-man.

Jonathan Butt rested, drank copiously, ate voraciously, and his big gaunt frame filled out.

Stores and equipment arrived and though the Scot recovered steadily Dilke chafed at the delay to the start of their mission.

Each day he spent time on the phone to the micro-training camp, questioning Settle on progress there, and each evening he fidgeted in Brymay's observation chamber and watched Bellamy's television.

The dossier of research notes on the tree disease aroused Jonathan Butt's interest and Dilke eagerly discussed the investigation with him during walks on the window-sill.

One morning they came to the plant, progeny of the office Busy Lizzie, which Bellamy had dumped in a water-filled glass jar and then forgotten. While the water lasted the plant had flourished; a skein of white roots almost filled the jar and a forest of leaves covered its serpentine stems. Hyacinthe and Mathew and Jonathan Butt stood beneath its branches and admired the massive pink blossoms which peeped from amongst its leaves.

The jar was almost dry. Only half an inch of water remained and the plant was wilting visibly.

'This plant has an unusual distinction, you know.' Jonathan Butt gestured to the root-filled jar. 'It's one of the few which can live in water alone and without soil.'

'The poor thing looks thirsty,' said Hyacinthe.

'Yes. It's rapidly dehydrating. It's a thirsty beast; you can actually see the water falling in the jar, and if you watch you'll see the branches sinking lower and lower.'

Hyacinthe stared, fascinated. 'But what does it *do* with all that water?'

'A plant is a living chemical factory. It mixes together the water from its roots and the carbon dioxide from its leaves, and with the help of sunlight it converts them into sugar.

'You see these stomata?' He indicated a number of vents, like green mouths, on the surface of the leaf. 'They open and close to regulate the flow of water in the plant. This is where carbon dioxide is inhaled and where unwanted water and oxygen is expelled.'

He sniffed at one of the stomata. 'At our size the expelled oxygen should give us quite a lift!'

With his knife he cut out a square block from the leaf and showed them its internal structure. Near the surface of the block the cells were like vegetable marrows packed tightly together in rows; the cells beneath were soft and spongy. Butt dug into a cell with the point of his knife and extracted a handful of translucent egg-shaped seeds.

The light shone through them and they glowed with a green fire.

'This is where plants get their colour. These chloroplasts contain chlorophyll which transforms light energy into chemical energy which in turn is used to manufacture carbohydrates – a process called photosynthesis.'

Jonathan Butt gave one of his rare smiles. 'It's even more complicated than it sounds – in fact the process has remained a mystery ever since Priestley discovered it in the 1700s.'

A drop of liquid fell and splashed down on to a leaf above them, interrupting Butt's discourse. They peered up and saw a green insect crawling sluggishly along a branch. It stopped, inserted its stylus into the branch and hung there, motionless. In a little while a drop of clear liquid formed at its rectum and grew in size until it fell to the ground beside them and slowly spread into a circular pool of viscous fluid.

Jonathan dipped a finger in the pool of liquid and tasted it.

'Sugar,' he said. 'Aphids tap the plant and it feeds them liquid sugar – and the plant's internal pressure forces some of it right through them.'

On the lowest branch, which almost touched the window-sill, hung a row of large gleaming, white excrescences. Butt reached up and tugged and twisted at one until it fell with a crash to the ground. It was roughly spherical and had a hard, slightly sticky surface. Butt stuck the point of his knife into it and split off some white crystalline flakes – Hyacinthe took a proffered piece and touched it with a tentative pink tongue.

'It's *sweet*!' she exclaimed.

Jonathan treated them to a second smile.

'That's Busy Lizzie's other claim to fame; she makes her own sugar lumps! You can put it in your tea if you have a mind.'

Dilke returned to the plant in the afternoon, armed with a machete.

He climbed up and found a small herd of aphids; picking out the fattest cow he struck at the junction between her head and thorax with his heavy knife. He kicked at the stubbornly clinging feet of the decapitated beast until it tumbled down through the leaves. The red eyes in the green head, still attached to the plant, shone with a sort of imbecile complacency and the honeydew poured up the hollow stylus and through the back of the head like a tap on a barrel of molasses. Dilke climbed down, cut steaks from its forequarters and took them home.

At suppertime Hyacinthe picked fastidiously at her share while Mathew and Jonathan ate their steaks with relish and agreed that the meat had a sweet flavour reminiscent of horseflesh.

After Hyacinthe had gone to bed, the two men took a walk. They climbed from the sill on to the sash of the window which overlooked the Embankment. Above the plane trees the floodlit mass of Battersea Power Station was visible. They had been discussing plans for the Canadian trip. Dilke gazed across the dark Thames at the smoke crawling from the enormous chimneys, then glanced at the man beside him.

'How do you feel, Jon?'

Butt did not turn his head. 'Right enough.' He raised a hand, its fingers outstretched, and slowly clenched it into a fist. His skin was no longer dry and scaly and the bones of his hand and forearm were now fleshed and heavy with muscle. 'Fit enough for work.'

PART TWO

Four

On the day of their departure Dilke hunted aphids and packed the refrigerator with meat. They made everything secure in the Brymay box then took supplies to last the journey to Canada and entered the gyro-transporter.

Bellamy flew to British Columbia via New York, picked up a hire-car in Vancouver and drove five hundred miles up the Alaska highway before turning on to a forest track leading to Redwater. After two days of travelling, the big Buick wallowed to a stop in front of the camp office.

There was not a log cabin in sight.

Redwater Logging Camp was a collection of pre-fabricated tin sheds and a water-tank on stilts; eminently portable and totally lacking the romantic appearance which Bellamy had expected.

The manager met him in his shirt sleeves; pale eyes shadowed by the peak of a blue baseball cap; a stubble of white bristles on a long jaw which stopped chewing momentarily to greet the visitor. The man preceded Bellamy into an office with a stove in the middle of a plank floor.

He jabbed a thumb. 'Meet Jacques Genet, my assistant.'

Genet bared horse-like teeth under a black Zapata moustache, and a moulting collie, its claws rattling on the floor, waddled over from the stove and squirmed cordially around the newcomer.

The room doubled as office and company wireless

station. The pine walls were plastered with forestry maps, bush-fire warnings and tractor-lubrication charts. A shotgun and a Winchester hung on pegs above a girlie calendar.

Bellamy's role was that of an English soil analyst. One more in a procession of tree doctors who had come to be shown the dying forest.

He stood by the stove holding a mug of stewed coffee, his other hand cupping the transporter in his coat pocket.

'Has the blight spread since you sent the map, Mr Ryan?'

'Naw! Not much. Maybe a coupla miles on the south border. It's where it'll start *next*.' The manager scowled. 'I had to fire thirty Jacks last fall.'

Bellamy's face showed incomprehension.

'Lumberjacks!' Ryan growled. He turned to his assistant. 'Hey, Jacques. You ready to fly this gentleman over to the ridge? Then go on and drop off the mail at the top camp.'

Bellamy set down his empty mug; his fingers sensed the minute vibration in the transporter deep in his car-coat pocket.

He coughed. 'I wonder, Mr Ryan, if I might, er, make a visit before we go?'

Ryan gave him a blank stare. Then he indicated a door at the back of the office. 'The john's through there.'

Bellamy made the transfer of his micro-passengers from the sphere to the matchbox while sitting on the lid of a chemical closet; then he returned to say goodbye.

The manager sat at his roll-top desk, concertina'd a stick of gum, nodded at Bellamy, and pushed the wad into his mouth.

Genet was waiting under the slowly revolving blades of a battered helicopter; as Bellamy approached the man dropped his cigarette in the mud, threw a bundle of mail into the cab and got aboard. Bellamy climbed in alongside him. The cabin interior was like an old estate wagon; a bundle of axe handles and some wire cable and drag-chains were piled up behind the seats. The pilot donned tinted glasses and put the blades into gear; the machine lifted off as if it would shake to bits and the old dog watched them go.

Brymay rested on Gilbert Bellamy's knee, held between finger and thumb, with its occupants strapped into the viewing-chamber seats. This was their first sight of Canada. The helicopter rose out of the circle of pines which surrounded the camp, and as it climbed above the dark trees a breathtaking view of the Rocky Mountains suddenly appeared. Jutting up beyond the intervening sixty miles of dense woodland, the peaks were capped with winter snow and glistened in the spring sunshine.

They turned in the air and travelled north, parallel with the mountains. The dark green carpet unrolled for mile after mile beneath them, patched with fresh green areas of reafforestation and scarred where timber had been felled.

The sky above was clear and blue, but some miles ahead a long, shallow cloud lay so low that it mingled with the tree tops. Suddenly they were flying through a grey fog, the blades spinning the vapour like a giant eggwhisk.

'This is it!' yelled the pilot.

Bellamy stared at him with surprise.

'We're here!' the man turned down a thumb.

The helicopter shot out of the white wall, trailing wisps of cloud behind it.

A glare of light from below filled the cabin. Bellamy and the micro-passengers stared down.

It was a white landscape.

Rank on rank of leafless, bone-white trees stretched for as far as they could see. The valleys were full of them and the hillsides and the ridges of the hills were covered with them.

Bellamy looked with awe at the desolate scene below.

To Dilke and Hyacinthe and Jonathan Butt, straining forward in their seats, the scale of destruction was frightful in its magnitude. A dead continent equivalent to nearly a million square micro-miles. An immense arboreal cancer of cosmic dimensions.

They flew on until the helicopter was above the very centre of the blighted area. The wall of vapour through which they had flown lined the southern perimeter of the circle; beneath them a river followed the line of a high ridge; Bellamy recalled the map of the area and recognized the place where the blight had originated and been marked with a cross. He nodded and smiled and indicated his wish to descend.

They dropped in a fast spiral, hung in clattering suspension for a moment while the pilot examined the ground below, then settled on a flat between river and ridge. The engine cut out and the blades clacked to a stop.

Gilbert Bellamy felt a little sick. The ringing in his ears was replaced by a silence so absolute that he wondered if he had lost his hearing and he pressed gently on an ear with his finger-tips.

The man at his side silently rolled shredded tobacco

48

between his palms and tipped it on to a cigarette-paper.

'And this is where it all began?'

'Right, Mac!' Genet ran his tongue along the gummed edge of paper, spat out of the open cockpit and rolled a humpbacked cigarette.

Bellamy produced a little shiny trowel and asked, 'Would you mind if I gathered some samples?'

'Help yourself, Bud.'

He drew deeply on the cigarette and watched Bellamy start up the slope.

A few trees lined the crest of the ridge and a giant dead pine, its roots locked deep in the stony ground stood at the highest point.

Bellamy laboured on, picking his way among fallen trees and carrying the matchbox as carefully as he could.

When he reached the big tree he was breathless. He sat wheezing on a tree root with his coat thrown open, wiped his steamed-up glasses and slapped crossly at the mosquitoes which had come up from the stagnant river. Then he knelt by the big root and cleared and levelled a patch of ground little bigger than a pocket handkerchief; he powdered the earth between his fingers, smoothed it, then patted it firm with the back of the trowel. He rested the Brymay box in the middle of the smooth patch, its window facing across the river to the south, and settled it with the gentle pressure of a big, fat finger.

Then he scratched up a handful of earth and dead pine-needles, added a fragment of tree bark, filled a small polythene bag with them and put it in his pocket.

He sat back on his heels and spoke softly to the matchbox: 'Goodbye, then. I will come for you in a month unless you advise the Vancouver agency before then.'

Bellamy fell silent and gazed solemnly at the box.

Down by the distant helicopter the man in dark glasses leaned against the machine and watched.

'Good luck, then. I must be off now.' Bellamy clambered slowly to his feet, dusted his knees and turned away. Dilke, Hyacinthe and Jonathan Butt left their seats and stood at the door of the matchbox and watched the big man descend the slope, touched by his evident concern.

The blades of the helicopter thrashed into a blur and it lifted off. As it rose its shadow remained motionless below it. Then as the machine flew north the shadow raced up the slope and over the hill in pursuit. The sound remained after the helicopter had disappeared, gradually getting fainter and fainter until it mingled with and was indistinguishable from the buzz of the mosquitoes which Bellamy's presence had attracted to the ridge. Long after he had gone the insects continued to zoom back and forth; landing on the tree root on which he had sat; standing head down where the man's hands had touched the root; then they left for good.

When evening came Dilke led the way indoors.

'We'll have an early night, Jon. I want to make an early start tomorrow—there's a lot to do in a short time.'

Five

Bellamy had settled them in a good spot but his attempt to smooth the area around the box had not been wholly successful: the particles of soil which had been dust in his great hands were like clods and boulders to Dilke and his companions. Yet the area was flat enough to prevent the unseen approach of predatory insects.

The box lay in a depression between a tree root to the east and rocks piled in the west. Now that the man and the machine had gone Brymay's occupants had little to remind them of their miniature size. Everything within the box was to their own scale. Bellamy's plain was a rock-strewn desert; the overhanging root was a looming geological outcrop; the boulders were a series of slab-sided cliffs. Even the heaps of grey pine-needles which had showered from the dead tree and lay in drifts between the boulders were like great logs piled up in valleys.

Only the pine tree itself could not be seen as a natural part of this miniature landscape – and yet its bulk was so immense, and their little valley lay so close to it, that the tree soon lost its identity in their eyes.

Hyacinthe sat on the ground with her back against the box wall and sunbathed, with her collar undone, her head laid back and her eyes closed.

'Getting a nice tan?' grinned Dilke.

Her eyes remained closed but a half-smile moved her lips.

'Wake up. I've got work for you to do. Your education has been sadly neglected.'

He set up a target and put Hyacinthe through an intensive course of crossbow shooting. Butt, who watched from the sidelines, was not impressed by crossbows. 'Why not have miniature firearms?'

Dilke lowered his bow. 'An insect has a nervous system with multiple control points and can't be knocked out by a single shot from a gun (have you seen a decapitated wasp cleaning its non-existent head, Jon?), but a crossbow bolt contains a killing venom which bursts inside the insect after the percussion-head has blasted a hole in its armour.' He grinned. 'We've simply improved on the insects' favourite weapon – *they* invented the poison dart!'

But Jon's preoccupation with research gave him no time for shooting and he frequently forgot Dilke's advice not to travel far unarmed.

He worked unremittingly: collecting soil samples from the plain and exploring the dark recesses under the root for fungus spores. He commandeered one end of the table for his research equipment and as the days passed the pages of his notebook filled with close-set writing.

Hyacinthe came running in one morning to say that there was a queer insect outside.

About a hundred paces from Brymay the men found a creature on its back with its legs in the air. It remained motionless; they watched it carefully for five minutes then cautiously approached it.

It was about seven millimetres long, a wingless, amber-coloured insect like a rather corpulent ant. Its belly was soft and wrinkled, smeared with a sort of white sludge and its six legs stuck up stiffly. It was unmistakably dead, yet the softness and moistness of its body suggested that it had died recently.

Its round head was armed with heavy jaws lined with smooth, white molars.

Hyacinthe stood well back and offered a classification: 'It looks like a white ant.'

'Looks like a termite, which is a rum thing as it has no right to be so far north as this.' Jonathan peered under the body. 'Look, Mathew, it seems to have been bitten or stung or something.'

There was a deep circular wound in the side of the creature's thorax just below the junction with the head.

They got ropes to haul it away before putrefaction set in and fouled the area, and while dragging the corpse over the rocky plain it tumbled over, belly down. The beast had no eyes, the round, white head was quite smooth except for a star-shaped formation or contusion on top. They burned it on a pyre of pine-needles at the edge of the plain.

Butt travelled farther and farther in his searches, sometimes taking a sleeping-bag and staying out at night.

Hyacinthe thought that from the beginning he had shown delicacy in his relationship with Mathew and herself; when he first joined them he took a bunk farthest from those in which they slept.

Hyacinthe thought that was nice of him.

'Och! It's just that he's a *dour* man—likes his Scottish privacy,' was Dilke's opinion. Yet the overnight absences did not seem wholly necessary and Dilke slowly grew to share Hyacinthe's view.

Hyacinthe watched the research with fascination. Jon Butt explained the techniques and she read his notes and gradually, as she became familiar with the work, she was able to help him.

Dilke volunteered to search for specimens for Butt's analysis. He left Brymay before sunrise one morning, wrapped up against the cold, wearing heavy boots and carrying a rucksack and field-glasses. He travelled towards the great wall of the tree until he reached the base of a boulder. A split ran up the rock face at an angle and Dilke slowly edged his way up, hanging at times by finger-tips and the toes of his boots. It was tricky and exhausting and he rested on a ledge below the summit. The gap between the boulder and the tree root was jammed full of pine-needles on to which he climbed from the ledge; then he leapt from needle to needle until he was able to scramble on to the root.

The sun rose. He searched for moss and lichen in the furrows of the root and travelled up and up towards the perpendicular wall. As he came nearer to the trunk and as the day brightened he saw that the bark of the tree was broken into a great criss-cross of furrows. The furrows ran at right angles to each other leaving irregular plates of bark about an inch square which projected in high relief.

The grey-white tree was tinged with green. Through his field-glasses he could see lichen growing in the recesses of the bark. He tucked the glasses inside his anorak, tightened his rucksack straps and started to climb. He was surprised at the ease of the ascent; it

54

was as if the tree had been made for micro-climbers; the vertical channels were open-sided chimneys wide enough to climb up, with good hand- and toe-holds. After each short climb he walked along the ledge on top of a block before climbing another channel, zig-zagging his way up the vertical face of the tree.

By mid-morning he reached the place where the lichen grew. It was multicoloured, though predominantly green, and he filled his sack until it bulged with the stuff. Then he rested on the ledge with his legs dangling in space, perched three feet up the face of the tree. He had climbed almost a thousand milli-metres, he was ravenous, his body ached and he was gloriously exhilarated by the climb in the bright spring sunshine.

Far below him the sun lit Bellamy's valley and glinted on the top of the box. BRYMAY read clearly like an advertisement painted on a flat, yellow roof.

He saw a movement at the door of the box. His glasses brought the two figures close. Jon Butt walked out carrying a chair, followed by Hyacinthe; he sat back-to-front on the chair with a white cloth around his neck and Dilke saw the glint of scissors in the girl's black hand. She pushed roughly, yet playfully, at the man's big head as she clipped at his hair and beard.

Dilke laughed silently: Fine mess she'll make with nail-scissors.

Twenty-five miles across the valleys covered with dead timber the vapour through which the helicopter had flown still rose—though now it seemed less dense, like smoke from a dying fire.

From his high position he could see many roots crawling from the base of the tree, twisting amongst the boulders and sinking into the stony ground. There was an unnatural stillness; the trees and the river were motionless and no life stirred.

It was indeed a dead world.

Dilke's buoyant mood was clouded by a vague feeling of frustration.

They seemed to be no nearer to finding the cause of the devastation. Butt's ceaseless investigation since their arrival had brought no success.

Dilke frowned. It seemed logical to use established research techniques – yet deep down he had no faith in them. To make new discoveries less conventional methods were needed. *Somehow* they must use the one advantage they had over the investigators who had preceded them – their day-to-day intimacy with the microscopic world which their miniature size gave them.

Dilke resolved to watch out for deviations in the normal patterns of nature which surrounded them.

Butt must continue with method and with logic. Dilke would try a little boy-scout observation – and intuition.

He ate lunch on the ledge before midday and had returned with his bag of lichen before supper.

Jon, who was pleased with the specimens, set to work preparing microscope slides and at his invitation Dilke looked down into the binocular microscope at a slice of magnified lichen.

'You're looking at a case of true symbiosis, Mathew, where two quite different organisms live in partnership together in a way neither could do alone. Lichen is algae surrounded by a casing of fungi; the algae have chlorophyll and provide energy from the sun –

56

and the fungi provide minerals and protection for the algae.

'Algae may be the earliest form of life on earth,' Jon added. '*Fossilized* blue-green algae 2,000 million years old have been found in this country. They live both on land and sea and are at the start of the food chain which feeds living things, from the simplest to the most complex forms of life.'

'Like us,' said Dilke.

'Naturally,' said Jon.

'At our size do we need a food chain? We should be able to eat this stuff straight.'

Jon agreed.

'Hyacinthe, when Jon's finished with his specimens we shall have green algae soup for supper!'

Dilke turned the pages of Butt's research notes and went on to examine the information with which they had originally been supplied.

'I see that your conclusions – or observations – are much the same as those we've been given already, Jonathan.'

Jon grunted and continued working at the microscope.

'Is it possible to examine the problem from some other directions?'

Jon pushed away the microscope. 'What other directions do you suggest?'

'I don't know, but is there much point in repeating the work?'

The row blew up without warning.

'You don't understand the scientific method, Mathew.'

Dilke slowly closed the book. There was a long pause.

'I *understand* that the Canadian and American labs have worked on this without result for almost four years now — using *precisely* the same methods you are using!'

Hyacinthe stared with bewilderment at the two men glaring across the table.

They sat very still for a long time. Then Jonathan Butt scraped back his chair, snatched his sleeping-bag from his bunk and walked out into the night.

'Oh, Mathew! *Why* did you have to do that?'

Dilke raised his shoulders, lifted his hands and let them fall back to the table. 'I really don't know. I didn't intend to.'

'Go after him!'

'No. It's the truth anyway.'

They went to their bunks and Dilke lay on his back in the dark with his eyes open and regretted it all.

Blind with rage Butt stumbled away from Brymay. The plain was ill-lit — but he would *not* return for a torch. And as he went south towards the open end of the valley his vision slowly accommodated to the poor light.

At last he came to the limits of the area which had been smoothed by Bellamy's god-like hand and halted by the blackened remains of the fire in which they had burnt the dead termite. Many, many micro-miles away, reflected stars shimmered on the river. Butt looked back. A tiny rectangle of yellow light marked the position of Brymay — and that damned man!

Butt cursed and left the comparative smoothness of Bellamy's valley, determined to lose sight of any reminder of Dilke's existence. He stumbled on down the rough slope for a few inches, then he climbed into his bag, scowled at the stars and moodily relived the quarrel.

When he awoke a mere shading of dawn augmented the starlight. Something moved on the plain. Something which was concealed from Butt by the rocks which surrounded his bivouac. He listened intently: the sound stopped; there was a short silence; then from the direction of the bonfire came the scrape and crash of charred pine-needles being shifted.

He slid from his sleeping-bag and crawled towards the sounds.

A big, humped shape burrowed at the heart of the dead fire, throwing up ashes and spreading the half-burnt stumps of pine-needles for an inch all round. It was too dark to see what species of insect it was but it was built like a tank and grunted like a wild boar.

Butt saw its armoured black head tugging at something. The thing was devouring the half-burnt remains of the dead termite; he heard the crack of shell-casing being crushed and the glutinous tearing of rotten flesh. The stink became unbearable. Butt was sickened, and he crawled backwards; his foot dislodged a fragment of rock which fell with a crash.

The beast's head jerked up and the sound of mastication stopped. Butt crouched down in the black shadows as the insect's twin antennae swivelled like radar above its raised head. Then it moved cautiously forward – Butt turned and ran.

He ran past his camp site to find a hiding-place amongst a pile of big, rounded pebbles which were half embedded in the ground – but the beast was

close behind. He saw an opening in the face of a
pebble and darted in. It was a dead end. Not the
opening to a refuge but a narrow, shallow split into
which he could hardly squeeze.

'Bloody Christ!'

Jonathan Butt was horribly afraid.

The huge brute now blocked the entrance to the
niche and clawed into its interior.

Butt dropped to the earth floor, twisted his body,
wedged a shoulder into the back corner, pulled a leg
tight to his chest and ducked his head on to the bent
knee. He was terrifyingly aware that the other leg
remained stuck out before him – within reach of the
scrabbling beast. But the insect did not search the
floor, its raking claws showered powdered rock down
upon him. Suddenly it withdrew. Butt heard it
blundering amongst the rocks, then the rip of fabric
as it tore at his sleeping-bag. It came again to his
place of concealment screeching with frustrated rage
and bit with iron-hard mandibles at the flinty
entrance.

Butt was paralysed with fear.

A spurt of liquid hit the rock above him and a
biting, acidic smell mingled with the hyena-stink of
carrion flesh.

Tears streamed from his eyes and he choked back a
fit of coughing with a cupped hand.

Then the creature backed away and its bulk no
longer obscured the light which kindled the eastern
sky. Butt sat wedged into his cranny long after the
sound of the departing insect had faded to nothing.

A burning sensation on the back of his hand
aroused him to violent activity. He cursed and
scrambled out, wiping his hand on his anorak. A

cluster of small yellow blisters were forming on the inflamed skin; he had nothing with which to treat them but he bandaged them in a makeshift way with his knotted handkerchief. Then he peered into the niche. A stench of formic acid filled the air. A splash of liquid had bleached the stone high at the back of the narrow cave – a farewell broadside from the departed predator – and was dribbling on to the floor where he had sat.

The terrifying escape from death which Jonathan Butt had experienced put his squabble with Mathew Dilke into perspective. Yet, though he knew that he should return to his companions, something in his nature prevented him from doing so.

First, he wished to recover from the nightmare attack before returning home. He left the area of broken ground near the fire and found a hollow at the edge of the plain, out of sight of the distant matchbox.

He lay in the sun all day, occasionally raising his head to look over the rise towards Brymay; thinking and re-thinking about the expedition, about his research and his relationship with his companions. His disregard of Mathew Dilke's advice always to carry a crossbow had almost cost him his life – the knowledge gave him a perverse feeling of irritation towards his adviser and a reluctance to meet him. But at dusk his acute hunger and the danger of a recurring attack from the night predator made further delay foolish.

Butt rolled up his tattered sleeping-bag, combed powdered stone from his hair with thick fingers and dourly set off for Brymay. He decided not to speak of his misadventure.

Dilke heard a faint sound and he walked from the inner room to the outer door.

Jonathan Butt was in one of the seats in the viewing chamber, looking through the perspex wall at the trees across the river, his sleeping-bag dumped in a seat at his side. Dilke sat down, the bag on the seat between them.

'I'm glad to see you back.' He smiled fractionally in the dim light. 'I was getting up a search party.'

'Aye! Captain Dilke.'

Dilke looked sharply at the dark figure sitting back with crossed legs and folded arms.

This was the first time the man had used either his title or his surname. He had seemed unaware of Dilke's role as micro-training controller – and Dilke had found this relaxing after the formalities at the training camp.

'I've had time to think about what happened last night,' Dilke said. 'You are right when you say I am not a scientist and not qualified to question your methods.' Butt remained silent. 'You must do your research in the way you think proper.'

Still Butt remained silent. But at last his dark shape hunched forward; his elbows on his knees and his big hands clasped together.

Dilke made a final, and oblique, attempt at conciliation: 'Can we not pick up where we left off? Hyacinthe has been worried.'

At last Jonathan Butt spoke. His accent had thickened and he spoke as if to the floor at his feet.

'You don't understand. Your judgment may be quite sound – I have had time to think too. At this place, with my qualifications and equipment, perhaps we *are* wasting our time.' Once more he lapsed into silence.

Slowly, the reason for the discord which lay between them grew clear in Dilke's mind: he had doubted the value of Butt's research from the start, yet he had concealed his doubts – had actually encouraged the Scot to continue by helping with the field-work.

Dilke recognized that he had been equivocal – that even his attempt at peacemaking had held an element of dissimulation.

'You think I have not been frank with you?'

Silence.

'That I have *never* believed in your research?'

Butt grunted.

Dilke paused, then forced himself to say the words: 'I'm sorry, Jon.' He paused again and added ruefully: 'Call me Machiavelli Mathew.'

Hyacinthe, who had crept in unnoticed, put out her hand and pressed his shoulder.

Butt surprised them with a new and almost obsessional interest in the crossbow, joining his companions in target practice and making such improvement that soon his marksmanship rivalled Dilke's own.

Dilke did not disclose his idea that the discovery of some freak element in their surroundings might lead them to the origin of the tree disease (the idea seemed too vague and unspecific to bear examination), but he induced Jon to continue his research, hoping that within the growing volume of data they would come upon a vital clue. He helped to look for specimen plants, finding lichen in damp holes and corners of the valley and a mushroom-like mould beneath pine-needles. And when they could find no more they decided to extend the search along the route he had taken on the day he had collected tree lichen.

Six

The men left after an early breakfast.

The first light of the day shone on the dew-wet boulder, tipping its rounded summit with pink. Dilke confidently led the way up its face, familiar with the crack in its surface and Butt followed torpidly at a little distance. As they climbed, the sunlight descended the wall to meet them, and when Dilke reached the ledge which led to the tree the rock was warm and dry. When Butt joined him on the ledge they continued their upward climb, curious to see what lay on the other side of the boulder.

They crawled up the last few millimetres and stood erect on the summit.

Dilke's eyes opened wide. Butt, who had yawned his way up the climb, stopped in mid-yawn. They were stunned into silence by what lay before them.

Before them stood the Alps!

A single, monumental rock — seven feet high — surrounded and buttressed by smaller rocks, jutted out of the hillside. Sub-arctic frosts had split the monolith into two peaks and sun, rain, ice and snow had weathered its mass into an incredible variety of geological shapes.

It was the Alps made small.

Since Bellamy had put them down in the valley they had experienced a reduced awareness of their true sizes: to Mathew Dilke and Jonathan Butt, who now squatted and stared up at the towering double peak, this truly was a mountain; with pinnacles, slabs, overhangs, ravines, terraces, buttresses and — a final touch of verisimilitude — a drift of bleached pine-needles sweeping down like a glacier from a hollow between the peaks into a pool of water at the foot.

At last Dilke turned his head away.

The eyes of the man beside him shone with an intense, almost rapturous look, which Dilke had never seen him show before; as if dazzled by the points of light which flashed from the quartz inlays on the flanks of the mountain.

Dilke peered over the edge of the boulder. A nick in its edge marked the start of a split which slanted down the boulder's face, providing a diagonal pathway to the shores of the distant lake.

He squeezed into the split, leaving his companion in rapt contemplation of the mountain-top. The wall and low roof were cold and wet with condensation, but the split increased in height till he could stand upright. Dilke stumbled downwards for half an hour. In places the split penetrated deep into the boulder; in its black recesses an eerie yellow-green light radiated from a soft fungus which clung to the rock; he carefully detached some and put it in his pack.

He looked down towards the lake.

Around him were dank walls, and fungi glimmered from the black interior behind him. In the chasm at his feet a shadow darkened the base of the mountain and the lake shore. The light reflected from the lake's irregular shape was as cold and bright as quicksilver.

Fall of the House of Usher, thought Dilke. He decided to go no further. He shivered and started the upward journey.

'Where does that lead to?' greeted Jon as Dilke wriggled on to the top of the boulder.

'Down to the lake shore, eventually, I suppose.' Dilke wiped his greasy hands on the smooth rock and lay back on its warm surface. 'But I've been as far as I want to; there's nothing much of interest.' He closed his eyes and enjoyed the warmth after his clammy journey. He dozed for a while, only half aware of his companion's movements.

Jonathan called his name.

Dilke raised himself on an elbow; his companion stood on the boulder's edge, looking down at the lake: 'You may be wrong. I think there *is* something of interest down there.'

Dilke joined Butt and looked down. As the morning had advanced the shadow across the base of the mountain had withdrawn until the lake and the rocky basin which contained it were bright with sunlight. The valley's mood had changed: now, points of light sparkled on the surface of the water and the shores, which had looked so sombre, were bright with meadows of green moss and purple lichen, softening the austere beauty of the whole landscape – and promising a harvest for Jon's analysis and Hyacinthe's cooking pots.

'It's too late to get down now but tomorrow we'll *surely* have a profitable day,' Jonathan Butt said with satisfaction.

Dilke suddenly wished to share the beauty and majesty of their discovery. 'Let's bring Hyacinthe, Jon!'

'Man, she'd never get down there. And we'll have our hands full getting stuff up.'

'No! I mean *now* — up here, to let her see!'

Hyacinthe was taking in the washing when Dilke hurried across the valley towards her. She stood, her arms full of shirts and sheets and called anxiously, 'Has something happened, Mathew?'

'No, lass. Leave your washin' and come awa' wi' me ... ' he used the brogue playfully to reassure her. 'We need your help ... ' He wished to give her no foreknowledge of their journey's purpose.

She put on boots, Dilke picked up binoculars and food and they left Brymay. Dilke climbed slowly and Hyacinthe followed carefully and neatly in his footsteps.

The sun had moved further west and it shone into their eyes as they crawled on to the top of the boulder. Blinded by the glare Hyacinthe at first noticed only the broad silhouette of Butt. 'Hello, Jon,' she called gaily. 'I thought you'd broken a leg!'

Then she saw the mountain.

They had first seen it flatly lit by the early sun. Lit from the side the effect was even more dramatic. She was speechless — just as they had been. Then she jigged to and fro on the boulder; laughing, pointing, putting into words the feelings they had felt. They watched her, grinning with pleasure at her uninhibited delight.

The men lay back on the rock and ate while

Hyacinthe stood with food in her hands examining the panorama before her.

'It's just like Switzerland!' she called.

'When were you in Switzerland?' Jon asked.

'I've seen pictures.'

After the meal Jon lay and methodically examined the dwindling sunlit areas of the mountain with the binoculars. She took them from him and playfully reversed them to look through. 'It makes everything look *tiny*!' she laughed. But Jon would not have the mountain diminished. 'That's not so. It makes things look farther off,' he chided, retrieving the glasses.

She wandered away and Dilke joined her and put an arm around her shoulders.

The twin peaks stuck up like ears. 'Like a cat's ears,' the girl said, 'or the devil's horns,' (and, indeed, the movement of the purple shadow across the mountain had given it a forbidding look).

'Or two breasts!' Dilke's hand spanned her breasts, the thumb and fingers stretched to touch each nipple. Hyacinthe glanced sideways at Jon's prone fingure, then frowned quickly at Dilke.

Dilke threw up his arm towards the mountain and declaimed: 'I name thee *Mount Hyacinthe*!'

The sun had moved behind the mountain-top but seams of quartz in the valley between the peaks picked up and deflected its rays into their eyes.

He called to Jonathan Butt, 'Or shall we call it Mount Kasama? The mountain with the jewelled breasts!'

'Mathew!' Hyacinthe protested. 'I think it's time we went home; it's getting dark.'

The sun reappeared. Now it was a hard, red ball moving across the gap between the peaks and for a moment it lay precisely midway between them. The effect was starkly symmetrical: a perfect circle between two triangles, like the sights of an enormous terrestrial gun.

Suddenly, and inexplicably, the three tiny people felt menaced; they turned away from the sombre black and red geometry of sun and rock and started the climb down to their own valley in the failing light.

Dilke forgot the mould he had collected in the morning until after supper. Then he put it before Jon for examination. It no longer glowed green and yellow but resembled putrified liver. Jon cut it open; the contents within the skin looked and smelled like overripe Camembert. He put it through a series of tests, looking more and more grave as the analysis proceeded. Finally he scraped the whole thing into a plastic bag which he dropped into Dilke's pack. 'Bury it, Mathew. Better still, burn it.' The faces of Hyacinthe and Mathew Dilke showed their surprise. 'It's *highly* toxic. Burn your pack as well,' he added.

Dilke made a small bonfire on the dark plain and watched till the flames subsided. He stirred the red embers and returned indoors to find that Jon had cleaned the table with an anti-toxin solution and had made a diluted solution for him to wash his hands in.

'If ever you want to polish us off, Hyacinthe, add a little of Mathew's mould to our diet. It's lucky for you the skin didn't break, Mathew. You have had two meals since you found it and you would almost certainly have transferred it from your hands to your stomach by now.'

*

Next day they went to the moss and lichen fields at the foot of the mountain.

Hyacinthe accompanied them as far as the top of the boulder and remained there while the men made their way down the split in the boulder's face to the lakeside. They came out on an area of barren rock and had a long walk to the collecting area. They packed different species of lichen into separate bags and dropped them into a big plastic sack, filling up the remaining space with green leaves of moss. The more succulent plants grew at the water's edge and Dilke crawled out on a mossy rock which overhung the lake — and saw something lying in the water.

It was an insect, lying on its back, deeply submerged, similar to the one they had found in their valley. There was a jagged hole in its abdomen, as if the pale belly had burst or been ripped open. Dilke leaned forward and looked intently at the wound; the water was as clear as glass; a swarm of tiny shrimp-like creatures whirled above the dead creature, apparently feeding on the contents of its gut.

Dilke hurried off to tell Jon Butt and found him standing waist high in moss looking at another dead insect. Like the one they had previously burned this one was also newly dead and without the odour of putrefaction. During the morning they found three more; one long dead, its tissues shrivelled to a stiff, brown casing, the crawling leaves of moss invading and growing through its carcass.

When the sack was full they started the return journey, discussing the mystery of the dead insects as they tramped towards the base of the boulder.

Jon slowly shook his head. 'I can't make it out! I'm

sure they're a species of termite. They don't *belong* here.'

Dilke glanced thoughtfully at his companion. Then why *are* they here? An indefinable sense of discovery stirred in his mind. What significance was there in the unnatural presence of these dead creatures? But was the presence of termites in Canada unnatural? Or was Jon wrong about the creatures' habitat? Or even their identity?

They had reached the rockface and Butt stopped and looked up. High on the lip of the boulder they saw the figure of the waiting girl. In an hour they would have joined her. Dilke turned to go but Jon remained standing with his big head laid back, squinting up at the rock.

'Let's take the direct route this time. It will cut the time by half.'

Dilke stared at the sheer face of the boulder with astonishment.

Jon dropped the plastic sack and slipped his rucksack from his back.

Dilke found his voice: 'You must be insane, Jon. We'll never climb that!'

The Scot tipped a collection of ropes, tent-pegs and a hammer from his rucksack.

'I've got the gear, Mathew. It'll be no trouble at all.'

Dilke stared into his companion's bearded and expressionless face. 'You sly beggar, Jon! When did you work this out?'

Jon gave no reply but stood back from the rock and examined it minutely. His eyes moved slowly up, tracking from side to side, until he shaded them from the glare of the sky at the top of the cliff; then he walked along its base for a dozen paces and repeated the examination. The rock looked unclimbable, but his deliberate and composed manner was both impressive and reassuring.

He briefly explained the use of the equipment, then walked to the foot of the cliff and started to climb.

For a heavily-built man Butt's climbing was fast and neat.

Dilke, who laboured in pursuit, needed a rest half-way. Then, lugging the sack behind him, he approached the last stretch of the climb with unconcealed relief.

Jon was waiting for him in the shadow of an overhanging promontory. 'Just another twenty millimetres and we'll be there, Mathew. But this is a tricky sod of an overhang.'

Dilke didn't like the vehemence of the comment.

Jon leaned right out and searched for a route. Dilke hauled up the sack and waited for guidance. Off to their right there was a nick in the overhang; the approach to it was across an apparently smooth and vertical wall; Jon moved delicately on to microscopic footholds, his hands outstretched as if attached to the rock surface by suction. He called in a muffled voice, 'There is a way but it'll mean a hand traverse.

'Slack off!'

Dilke gave him two millimetres of rope and watched him step off the last foothold without hesitation and swing from hand to hand across the wall till he was below the groove in the bulging promontory. He plunged a hand into a hidden crack, inserted a peg above his head with his free hand, took the hammer from within his shirt and hammered the peg in.

Then he worked his way up hammering in pegs with abandon and climbed out of sight.

Dilke heard a murmur of voices from above.

A voice called faintly: 'Free the bag, Mathew.' The released bag soared away, scuffing and spinning across the rockface, then swung to and fro till it hung motionless before being hauled over the lip of the boulder. Dilke felt very lonely.

He sat beneath the overhang sweating gently and started a mental countdown from ten before starting his fly-on-the-wall act.

He stepped out sideways. A series of minute footholds supported only his toes; his heels ached with the strain. From the last toehold he prepared to transfer from feet to hands. He leaned into the wall with his cheek against the rock and tried another countdown – which gave him ten seconds to view the tremendous plunge of the cliff below and time for his legs to develop a violent attack of muscle shake.

He stretched out and grasped the first hold. He was spread across the rock in a sort of diagonal splits, supported by one hand and one foot. Grunting at the pain in his muscles he pushed off with the foot in a desperate effort to start the hand traverse; both his sweating hands slipped off the holds.

Like the bag, he swung across the rockface and the rope scraped along the cliff-top showering him with dust and pebbles. He heard Hyacinthe scream.

The rope, which had kept a light tension, pulled and stretched but held him.

Jon Butt's shout came down, faint but calm, 'Are you all right down there?'

Dilke was too busy coughing up dust to reply.

The rope was pulled up as if by a winch. Dilke's

fright changed to mortification at finishing the climb like a hauled sack. He reached the pegs, climbed them hand-over-hand and scrambled over the edge on all fours. He staggered to his feet then promptly sat down.

Seven

The fleshy leaves of the moss when sliced, chopped and boiled, went well with the sweet aphid meat.

During supper Dilke brought up the subject of Jon's newly revealed climbing skill. He felt that his ordeal on the rockface was a tit-for-tat for his own previous lack of candour.

Jon admitted, with a smile, considerable knowledge of mountaineering.

'I've climbed since I was small. My mother wanted me to be a scholar but I was a perverse child and went rabbiting and climbing with crofters' sons instead of doing homework. The blacksmith's son and I climbed up the inside and then down the outside of our local watch-tower. Seventy feet of rotten stone which came away in handfuls. We watched club climbers on the Cairngorms, then made pitons in his father's forge and went climbing with his mother's clothes-line. The rope broke halfway up a face and I fell sixty feet. I was lucky, considering. Only concussion and broken wrists ... '

Dilke had pulled on a thread which ran through Jonathan Butt's life and over supper he told them more than they had learned since he first joined them.

He had taken geology at Edinburgh, and had spent his vacations on Welsh and Scottish mountains and climbing with joint student teams in Europe and Russia.

Dilke asked, 'Govorichye po Rousske?'

Butt answered with a stare.

'You didn't pick up the language?'

'Only "Bloody Niet"! I didn't take to the Russians. They all want to be heroes, I didn't like sharing the same rope. They had strict rules against smoking and drinking – but they did both on the quiet.'

They talked until late and it was midnight before they went to their bunks.

Dilke spoke in the dark. 'How does a Scot get a name like Butt?'

Jonathan Butt sounded defensive. 'I had an English great-grandad, a horse-dealer from Northumberland who traded in Fifeshire, married a McDonald. The name came down from son to son. I'm only one-eighth English.'

Dilke was not deterred from climbing. He returned next day to the scene of his discomfiture and ascended the face of the boulder again, completing the climb without loss of dignity.

Then the men stood on the boulder summit and prepared for the easy descent into Bellamy's valley. Dilke coiled a rope and looked down on the matchbox roof. Hyacinthe was not in sight.

He turned towards the south and a distant movement caught his eye. A slender, grey, snake-like creature had crawled on to the tree root and was sliding slowly up it towards the trunk of the pine. And yet its movement was not snake-like: it did not writhe, it rippled.

Dilke looked quickly at his companion. Jon had binoculars on the creature.

'Pine caterpillars,' Butt muttered and handed over the glasses; through them the snake became a herd of caterpillars travelling nose to tail and, as the column advanced, more and more caterpillars appeared over the curve of the root. Occasionally the leading one stopped, bringing the whole column to a halt, raised the forepart of its body and swung its head this way and that. The root formed the high eastern wall of the valley and where it curved up sharply to meet the tree trunk the first caterpillar hesitated, raised its body and darted its head to and fro as if seeking a different way. Then it turned, led its followers from the crest of the root and crawled down vertically on to the valley floor.

To the micro-men, watching from above, the procession swayed like a wagon-train across a boulder-strewn plain.

From the leading caterpillar to those which appeared in the distance the composite creature was ten feet long – and still it grew in length. Now the leader moved along the middle of the valley – Dilke and Butt scrambled down the crack in the face of the boulder and raced towards the matchbox.

They were too late. An unbroken line of plodding, inch-long caterpillars separated them from Brymay.

The huge elephant-grey beasts trudged past in a haze of dust and rattling stones. The bristles on their backs glittered like bayonets in the sun; their flaking hides were folded and creased on their shrunken carcasses; at each step of their many legs, slits gaped in their concertina'd skins and revealed ulcerated flesh beneath.

A thin loop of saliva swung from each caterpillar's mouth and fell to the ground between its feet, adding another dribbled thread to the milky network which marked the pathway of those which had gone before.

Deprived of living, green pine-needles, they subsisted on the hard, dead needles which had fallen from the stricken trees.

The caterpillars were dying of starvation and exhaustion.

A score of ants suddenly appeared on the tree root and attacked the column.

Few living things remained in the dead forest, but small tribes of primitive ants had survived its death — aboriginal creatures, freed by the extinction of their more sophisticated and dominant cousins to come out of their holes and corners to hunt for food in daylight.

The savage brutes descended to the valley floor to overturn and butcher the squirming caterpillars. A haze of dust rose around the struggling creatures and floated towards the micro-men. A familiar smell stung Jonathan Butt's nostrils. The smell of formic acid; reviving a nightmare memory of huge insect claws raking the dark walls of a cave where he crouched in terror …

Butt turned and, followed by Dilke, ran to the foot of the boulder and hid amongst the pebbles at its base.

The marauders made no attempt to dismember their prey and carry it off, but — avoiding the bristling spines on the backs and sides of the caterpillars — they ripped out the soft bellies and ate the trembling flesh on the spot. Oblivious of the fate of their companions, the column moved on.

A shadow swept across the valley.

The sun was blotted out.

A hurricane of wind blew.

Dust spiralled upwards and rocks were thrown against the boulder and showered down around the crouching men.

Hurricane gave way to earthquake as the clawed feet and gleaming shanks of a huge bird crashed into the valley. The spread wings of a carrion crow made a black canopy, the quills of its flight-feathers curved overhead like the roof struts of a massive stadium. Dust clouds obscured the scaly feet and whirled around the twin columns of its legs. Its great leaden beak hammered a dozen times at the ground then with a flip of its wings it bounded on to the tree root and pick, pick, picked the root clear of ants.

The bird cocked its head, searched the valley with a yellow eye, then launched into a long, swooping dive towards other crows at the river's edge.

The two men staggered to their feet, bruised by flying stones, and looked with astonishment at what lay before them. The once-level plain had been trampled into a shambles of sand and rock. The ants had vanished; a few caterpillars had been crushed underfoot, others had been swept off their pathway and tumbled about the valley. The strand of silk had stretched but not broken and lay twisted and half buried under debris.

Dilke and Butt beat dust out of their clothes and gathered up their climbing gear, then hurried towards Brymay.

Hyacinthe stood in the darkened interior with a crossbow aimed at the doorway. Dilke took the weapon from her trembling hands and they joined Butt in the viewing chamber. The first batch of caterpillars had disappeared down the southern slope but those which had been thrown off the path could be seen searching erratically for it, twisting and turning their bodies and peering myopically about. Each one found the thread at last and shambled after its vanished companions.

Later, the main body of caterpillars descended from the root and filed past Brymay in an unbroken line. Hyacinthe and Jon and Mathew Dilke watched them through the perspex window, mesmerized by their rhythmical movement. When it was too dark to see they went in for supper and listened to the muffled sound of marching feet.

After supper Dilke returned to the observation chamber. Now it was silent and nothing moved in the darkness. There was a touch of frost and the stars sparkled with cold light. Points of golden light glowed at the end of the valley like the embers of a spent bonfire. Through binoculars the lights bobbed and winked interminably as if they were lanterns carried by a multitude of people. Dilke called Hyacinthe and Jon and they left the matchbox carrying torches and crossbows.

The path which had started as a single cord of saliva trailing from the cleft lower lip of the lead-caterpillar was now a highway of silk which gleamed in the starlight. As they walked along its cushioned surface and came near to the lights, a strange murmuring and rustling filled the air.

They moved with more and more caution.

Dilke flicked on his torch. A great grey mound of pine caterpillars overflowed each side of the silk roadway. Hundreds and hundreds of them, huddled together for warmth, motionless but for the uneasy movements of those on the edge of the mound who tried to push their way into the centre. Their multiple eyes shone with a steady radiance.

81

Next morning the pine caterpillars had gone from Bellamy's valley. Hyacinthe and the two men walked on the road at dawn, skirted the vast midden of grey droppings which marked the night camp, and looked down the slope towards the river.

The caterpillars had travelled far but were still in sight, moving generally to the south but deviating wildly to east and west on the rough ground. The single column had now broken into short lengths of fifty to a hundred individuals, some of which were quite still; others travelled with a hardly perceptible movement, lurching painfully along their shining white highway to final collapse and inevitable death – for the nearest living trees were across the river, twenty-five miles away.

'I cannot watch. They are like dying elephants,' said Hyacinthe, and she turned back along the road.

'Why didn't the crow eat them?' asked Dilke.

'Their spines make them distasteful and they secrete a poison,' said Jonathan Butt. 'Only cuckoos can stomach them!'

The weather, which had steadily grown warmer as spring advanced, became changeable. Cold squalls of rain were driven from the west and dropped into the valley, exploding on the roof of Brymay and pock-marking the surrounding plain with craters. Afraid that the plain might be flooded, trapping them in the matchbox, they camped on higher ground in the shelter of the tree root.

A blazing sun dried the valley floor on the following day, making the exterior of the steel box burning hot and forcing them to sleep outdoors as the box interior was oppressively stuffy. As they lay side by side under the stars Jon revealed a plan he had made.

He wished to climb Kasama.

'Surely such a climb would need a team and a series of supply camps,' Dilke said.

'No. I have worked out a route which two men could climb in two or three days – if they went hard at it ...'

Dilke gave no reaction.

'We would name the peaks Dilke and Butt ...' Jon added.

Dilke turned on his side and propped his head on his hand to look at his prone companion. Hyacinthe lay between them in her sleeping bag, her features almost invisible in the darkness. He examined the idea carefully. It was an attractive idea which would exercise his growing climbing ability. But there was an obstacle: Bellamy would arrive soon to pick them up.

'I don't want to be left alone, Mathew,' Hyacinthe said softly.

Dilke spoke again after a silence: 'There isn't time. Sorry, Jon. Gilbert Bellamy will be here in a few days.' Jon lay without a sound, as if asleep, but Dilke sensed his silent disappointment.

Dilke watched the moon float out from behind the great pine tree and an idea slowly grew in his mind. He could send micro-men to this valley as part of their training – a final toughening up – Butt could be in charge and could climb Kasama to his heart's content ...

Dilke woke at about five. The valley and the tree were in tones of grey, shrouded by a light mist.

Something had wakened him. He lay and waited for the sound, breathing lightly and watching his breath condense in the cold morning air. A rattle of stones in the distance grew louder. Dilke turned his head and looked into Hyacinthe's wide eyes.

Jon sat up suddenly and stared towards the tree. A huge shape came from behind it.

The bear walked into the valley between the boulder and Mount Kasama. It put a great forepaw on the boulder; stood erect, snuffled with wet, black nostrils then dropped down out of sight. They heard its enormous lapping tongue, then the sound of its departure along the crest of the hill.

Before the noise of its movements had ceased they heard the approach of another creature. The clatter of rocks and the crack of broken branches grew louder. The ground moved beneath them. A shadow filled the valley.

Two colossal paws stood on the tree root. The mother of the thirsty cub stood above them and the rank smell of her breath and her great body filled the air. She swayed from side to side, gaunt from hibernation and from feeding her cubs; hanks of moulting hair hung from her flank. She turned to the tree, reared on to her hind legs and stretched up to sharpen her claws on the bark. A shower of fragments fell around her, crashing down into the valley where they lay in their sleeping-bags, too petrified to move.

The she-bear stepped across the valley, blotting out the sky, and followed her cub.

They scrambled out of their bags, ran across the valley and climbed to the summit of the boulder to watch the bears.

84

The cub, which was digging into an open-ended log for a wild bees' nest, was joined by a larger cub and relinquished the nest to him. The empty combs powdered under his scrabbling paws and covered him in dust; he sneezed, then chased after his mother and sister.

The bear searched for fish in the river, her cubs tumbling around her in the shallows.

From the boulder near the top of the ridge the enormous creatures now seemed diminished: but the lake at the foot of Mount Kasama was dry and a great paw had crushed the meadows of moss.

The bears disappeared round a bend in the river.

Eight

Since the appearance of the bears – forcing on them a recognition that their valley and mountain and lake were only tiny replicas of real things – the men had given up climbing.

There was a feeling of inertia in the camp.

Jonathan and Hyacinthe filled in time before Bellamy's arrival by idly combining and collating the research notes.

Butt's conventional research had not disclosed the cause of the blight which threatened the North American forests, and though Dilke still felt that a less obvious and more oblique approach might have turned up something new his own constant watchfulness had revealed nothing tangible.

Raglen's parting words – 'You may find nothing. It's a long shot' – did little to lessen Dilke's depression.

Two nights before the pick-up date they lay in the valley and looked at the quarter-moon hanging in the mesh of dead branches. As Dilke lay, close to sleep, his eyes dazzled by the moon's cold brilliance, he saw a wisp of smoke appear at the tip of a high branch.

The smoke grew in volume and drifted away on the wind. Dilke placidly gazed at it, accepting its existence as if it were in a dream.

'Mathew.'

Butt's insistent voice brought Dilke awake. 'Do you see it, Mathew?'

The smoke blew across the face of the moon, darkening the valley. 'What the hell is it, Jon? A fire?'

Their voices wakened the girl; the smoke filled her with vague alarm. The men had left their sleeping-bags and were standing at a little distance with their heads back, talking in an animated way about the bizarre phenomenon.

'Can it be a fire, Jon?' Dilke brought together the bunched fingers and thumbs of both hands then sprang them apart. 'A sort of spontaneous combustion?'

Butt shook his head in doubt, then scrubbed at his beard with the palm of his hand. 'Maybe the cellular structure is breaking down—these dead trees are very brittle—and some sort of vacuum-pull by the wind is dragging the powder out ...' he spoke without conviction. 'I don't know. I'll be damned if I do!'

The smoke stopped pouring from the branch after an hour. They watched the last wisps float from the tip and follow the long body of cloud which drifted to the south and they discussed it long after it had disappeared.

'It's a freakish damn mystery!' Butt finally summed up. 'This is something new. I wish I could get some particles for analysis ...'

The baffling appearance of the smoke left Mathew Dilke in a state of sleepless excitement.

Here was an event which defied rational explanation, one observed by himself and his two micro-companions alone – for no previous investigators had reported such a happening.

At last he turned on his side and closed his eyes.

Before he fell asleep an inspired thought came to him. He smiled: he would postpone the pick-up and they would climb the tree and they would solve the mystery.

When Dilke woke the memory of the smoke was dreamlike. But it was a dream they all shared.

And when he looked at the immense pine tree – towering above him Everest high – his bold plan of the night seemed absurd.

Yet the idea stayed persistently in his mind, filling him with a nervous exhilaration.

He turned to Jonathan Butt.

'How high is Everest?'

Butt did not answer.

'How high is Everest, Jon?'

Butt's eyebrows drew up in surprise. 'About thirty thousand feet.'

Near enough to the height of the pine in micro-terms. 'How would you like to climb it, Jon?'

Butt flashed a bewildered look at the girl, then stared at Dilke.

'What *is* the matter, Mathew?' Hyacinthe said.

He grinned over their heads and nodded at the tree. '*There* is Everest!'

Butt looked up at the branch from which the smoke had come, then his gaze moved slowly down to the base of the great tree and he examined the regular pattern of its bark.

He turned his head and looked into Dilke's eyes.

'Aye!' His lips were compressed in a tight smile and his head nodded slowly. 'It would be *our* Everest.'

Dilke spoke to Vancouver and put back the pick-up date by six weeks.

PART THREE

Nine

April 4th. Dilke slammed the matchbox door shut at dawn.

A crow's feather lay half-buried at the northern end of the valley, its quill stuck in the valley floor, its feathered tip touching the root of the tree. They ascended the giant stepladder of black vanes, scrambled on to the curve of the root, then followed the way which Dilke had travelled when he climbed the tree for lichen. Each had a rucksack and crossbow and Butt carried the tent in a plastic sack. They roped together at the foot of the tree with Jon in the lead and climbed steadily throughout the day. The vertical and horizontal grooves between the inch-square plates of bark made progress easy—the rough surfaces of the vertical channels provided good holds and the horizontal ledges were convenient resting places.

Hyacinthe climbed happily and securely between the two men.

They slept on a ledge, their sleeping-bags roped to pegs hammered into the bark. They had climbed six feet.

April 5th. They were stiff after the first day and now climbed more slowly and methodically. The jagged grooves which the bear had ripped in the tree gave variety to the ascent. They scrambled up the edges of clawed-out channels and came to the highest scratch mark at ten feet. A slab of bark hung by a few fibres from the tree concealing a deep recess with space to pitch the tent and as it was late afternoon they decided to climb no further. The site which had seemed so spacious and sheltered turned out to be less good than their rather precarious bivouac of the previous night. The hulk of bark swung in the breeze, disturbing their sleep with its intermittent thudding against the tree.

They looked forward to reaching the first branch – they could camp in its fork; and beyond it they could ascend from branch to branch.

April 6th. Hyacinthe climbed with graceful non-chalance and they dispensed with the rope. Now they made faster time; though Jon, his pack augmented by the tent, sometimes got jammed in the narrower chimneys; Dilke and Hyacinthe heard his curses drift up from below.

Finally he worked out a way of transporting the load by attaching a line to it, then climbing ahead and drawing it after him.

April 8th. Twenty-five feet up the tree they reached the first branch.

Fine particles of dust and bark had washed down its shallow gulleys, making a level plateau in the crotch between branch and trunk. Here they pitched the tent and had supper: meat, and the lichen which grew plentifully on the tree.

They had discovered different varieties of lichen as they ascended, which gave them a changing diet. 'We could live on it if we had to,' said Jon.

They sat by the fire and reviewed their progress. In five days they had ascended almost a quarter of the tree. Though strenuous the climb was not specially arduous – Butt gave it a B for Boring – and with an average of 1,800 millimetres a day they would reach their destination in less than a fortnight. They looked up hopefully for a sign of the mysterious smoke, but the moon had not risen and the branches were visible only as black spaces in the constellations of the stars.

April 10th. After six days of sunshine British Columbia was a vast hot-plate which heated the cold Pacific air and made it rise in moist clouds up the sides of the inland ranges.

During the morning climb Butt looked repeatedly towards the high barrier of the Rockies where, caught between the Pacific airflow and opposing prairie winds, vapour piled up in immense stratospheric thunderheads.

Butt, who took the lead after their midday break, urged them to push on, and he watched grimly as high velocity winds cut off the tops of the black clouds and swept them back.

It was suddenly cold.

'The weather's on the turn,' Butt shouted down. 'Hurry up!'

They joined him and crouched beside him on a ledge, buffeted by the wind and peering up at the sky from beneath the overhang. 'We're not going to make it to a branch,' grunted Butt. 'Best to get round to the leeward of the tree and sit it out.' He set off at a crouching run along the ledges, jumping across the gaps between the slabs of bark – his reckless speed showing his anxiety more clearly than his words.

The light was failing quickly.

The advancing cloud mass, now flattened into a huge black anvil shape, voided fifty million volts of electricity and split the sky with lightning — illuminating the dead forest with blinding clarity. Thunder jarred their tree and when it had growled away beneath the cloud ceiling they heard the hiss of approaching rain.

Butt had vanished.

Hyacinthe shook uncontrollably and Dilke dragged her across the gaps.

Driving rain hit the tree with a shattering roar, exploding into fine vapour which swirled under the protective overhang. At first the dry mass of the tree, heated by the prolonged hot weather, absorbed the water, but as the bark became saturated flood water poured down the channels making their leaps from ledge to ledge more and more hazardous.

Dilke began to curse the absent Butt and was about to jettison their packs when a shrill whistle from ahead signalled them on.

Butt crouched at the entrance of a narrow black hole.

They bundled Hyacinthe in, threw their gear after her and scrambled in themselves, then sat panting for breath, their minds empty of everything but dazed relief at being safe.

Rain mixed with hailstones streaked horizontally across the sky. It was as if a million siege guns pounded the tree. Lightning and thunder followed each other interminably. They sat in a row with their hands pressed against their ears.

The darkness of the storm shaded into the darkness of night.

Their overwhelming relief at finding shelter was slowly overlaid by the daunting realization that they must spend the night in the narrow cave.

Soaked with rain and sweat, they were chilled by the cold night air even though huddled together for warmth. Their ankles and knees ached with the strain of squatting on the sloping floor – down which they might slide into space if they dozed off to sleep. They fidgeted and shifted position for an hour, listening to the downpour sighing in the valleys below. Jon muttered and grumbled to himself then took his hammer, hammered pegs into the walls and wove a catch-net across the cave entrance. He pulled the tent from its waterproof sack and spread it on the floor beneath them; Hyacinthe lay on the folded tent, enveloped in the sack, and the men sat side by side and leaned forward against the net.

Dilke slept fitfully. Waking in the dark to hear torrents of water rushing down the tree, comforted by the feel of Hyacinthe's body against his back.

April 11th. After a black eternity the cave entrance appeared as a grey triangle. Water flowed in translucent curtains over the cave's mouth.

Dilke dozed off for an hour and when he woke the flow of water had almost stopped. A drop formed at the top of the cave's opening, grew into a trembling orb, hung like a great transparent pear, then fell.

A second, a third, a fourth drop followed the first.

Ten, twenty, thirty, forty, Dilke was hypnotized by the regular pulse of water. Each drop was a huge lens in which images of the fast-brightening world outside appeared upside down.

The sun rose.

Its rays — refracted into a spectrum of colours by a waterdrop — flared into the cave and filled it with moving patterns of red, yellow and green, blue and indigo and violet.

The cave had a curiously unnatural shape with a sloping floor, and smooth walls which converged to meet overhead; the floor and walls narrowed to a point at the back. Dilke turned to examine it, then looked down at Hyacinthe, who lay with strands of hair across her face, the sack pulled up round her neck and head. Her eyes opened and they exchanged yawns. She smiled.

'Good night?' he asked quietly.

Hyacinthe closed her eyes and nodded.

'Warm?'

She nodded again.

During the night Dilke had withdrawn his arms from his sleeves and folded them across his body to keep warm. He pushed out a hand from within his anorak and with a conjuror's gesture presented a glucose lozenge between finger and thumb. 'Breakfast?'

She smiled, opened her mouth like a child and he popped it in.

Butt sat impassively watching a raindrop evaporate in the sun, the stiff fingers of his big hands hooked together, his arms resting on the top rope.

The inverted image of sun and mountains grew sharper and smaller as the sphere shrank, then only a damp patch remained at the top of the cave's entrance.

It was a glorious morning with a clear blue sky, bright and fresh, washed clean by the rain. Dilke and Butt climbed down on to the ledge and hobbled about like old men, groaning at the cramp in their legs; then they all roped up and Dilke led the way cautiously up the first chimney. In the shadows the tree was still wet and slippery with melting sleet. At noon he scrambled on to a ledge and discovered a cave which was so like the one in which they had spent the night that it was as if he had experienced a shift in time and had slipped back twelve hours.

When his companions joined him they all stared at the triangular opening of the cave.

Jon walked away along the ledge, then stopped and called them; he had found a row of three more caves, each one the same shape, size and depth.

Dilke leaned in and examined them with wonder. 'They're identical, Jon. Identical!'

Butt sat in a cave entrance and uncapped his water-canteen. 'I thought for half the night about that shape ... ' he drank from the flask and wiped his mouth. 'This tree has been climbed. These recesses are the marks of climbing irons. It's a shame they're not more comfortable, we could have camped in them all the way up.' He stepped forward, looked down and pointed to a tangle of dark branches on the slope below. 'This tree was topped before it died — you see how dark the crown is.'

'But why would they do that?' asked Hyacinthe.

'They must have started felling here. They top the

highest tree then attach tackle to it and winch timber out of awkward lies; we do it in Scotland too.'

April 12th. The carrion crow dropped on to the dead branch with a clatter of wings and clutched it with claws which wore spats of dried mud.

It gave a gutteral croak, scratched its head with a taloned foot, then cleaned mud from its beak and from its belly feathers.

Plunging its head under half-raised wings it ran its bill rapidly down the length of each flight-feather; twisting its body it nibbled and teased its disarranged tail-feathers into order; taking beakfuls of oil from the gland on its rump it meticulously lubricated its black plumage till it gleamed with purple and green highlights. All this to a soliloquy of gargles and sinister chuckles.

Its toilet finished, it flapped its wings noisily, held them on high for a moment then folded them to its heavy body.

The crow was only a foot away from the camp that they had set up in the fork of the branch.

The wind from the huge wings tore out some of the tent-pegs and smoke from the cooking-fire blew in their faces.

From the moment the bird arrived Hyacinthe and Jonathan and Mathew Dilke crouched around the fire in frozen silence and stared up at its enormous bulk, astonished at the power and vigour of its movements.

It bent its head and stropped its beak with great speed and energy on the branch.

Then it saw the fire: a glowing spot no bigger than a

match-head. It shuffled two inches nearer and stared at it curiously.

They cowered down as the great head came nearer and nearer. There was a reptilian quality about the bird's unwinking eyes and its scaly legs that was both repulsive and terrifying. The bristling feathers which concealed the breathing holes vibrated with the passage of air, grey lice clustered on the lower borders of the creature's eyes and at the corners of its tar-black beak.

The huge head lifted, then drove down.

The tip of the great beak crashed into the fire, obliterating the flames and scattering ashes in all directions. The impact bounced them into the air and sent them sprawling. They scrambled up, dived into the concealment of the tent and lay in a panting heap.

The glowing object had vanished leaving only a wisp of smoke, but the bird had seen the three small insects scuttle out of sight.

From within the tent they heard the creak and scrape of giant feathers and the whistle of breath through the crow's nostrils. Dilke peeped out. The bird's bright eye was only a few inches from the tent.

He reached back for a crossbow which hung from the tent pole then shakily brought the weapon to his shoulder and cocked it.

The bird swivelled its head and examined the tent with its other eye; a transparent third eyelid flashed across the great yellow orb.

Dilke shot two bolts into the eye. One went through the black pupil into the lens, the second pierced the eyeball and fragmented deep inside the bony eye socket.

The screeching bird shot up and crashed into overhead branches.

The tent collapsed in the slipstream of its flapping wings and when they had crawled from beneath it the crow was performing demented aerobatics at five hundred feet.

Seeing the bird cross the river in a series of crazed loops and somersaults, a flock of crows which was digging on the mud-flats rose to intercept it. Incensed by its eccentricity, the crows attacked it with furious rage, punching it about the sky with the violence of their assault. Twisting and turning to escape the slashing claws and stabbing beaks the stricken creature flew back towards the pine. The fluid within its eyeball — now wholly corrupted by the venomous contents of the crossbow bolt — seared the inner membrane of the eye.

The great bird screamed.

A rage of pain drove it on with extraordinary velocity.

It hit the top of the ridge like a black bomb and exploded into feathers.

Its persecutors crouched in the surrounding trees and scolded their victim, then, one by one, they returned to the riverside to dig for ragworms.

Hyacinthe found the battered metal cooking-pot amongst the scattered ashes and Jon reshaped it with his big hands. But fright had destroyed their appetites and they went to bed without supper.

April 13th. Dilke came to the lip of a great cavity, a

black mouth two hundred millimetres high, its edges polished and stained by generations of nesting birds.

Hyacinthe joined him and they walked cautiously in.

They heard the sound of lapping water and accommodating to the darkness, saw that the old nest-hole was filled to the brim with water. The surface of the lake bristled with the snorkel tubes of mosquito larvae and feathers floated like black galleons at its edge. Bird droppings encrusted the lakeside and the air was sour.

A gravid mosquito flew in, circled the cavern overhead, then descended to the surface of the water to lay eggs which floated down like cream in black coffee.

'Hello-lo-lo-lo-o-o-o!'

Jon's shout filled the vault with echoes.

With eggs still squirting from its ovipositer the insect took off and whined out of the tree. Jon stood at the cave entrance, they saw him duck as the big insect zoomed over his head then he bent at the water's edge and drank.

They made Camp Ten in the angle between branch and tree late in the evening and had supper in the warm light of the western sun.

Jonathan Butt had been more than usually mono-syllabic during the last part of the climb. Now he put his food to one side and unpacked the tent. They had devised an effective, if unconventional way of using the tent fabric, stretching and pegging it over a trench between two ridges of bark; then sleeping in line beneath it.

After they had settled for the night Hyacinthe
heard the men talking quietly, then the sound of
Butt crawling from under the canopy and walking
away up the slope of the branch.

'What is it, Mathew?'

'It's Jon, he's got a touch of diarrhoea. It must be
the water he drank at the mosquito pool.' He sat up.

'Are *you* all right?'

She heard him shuffle out of his sleeping-bag. His
hand came down on her face and his lips touched
the corner of her mouth, she raised her chin and they
kissed upside down.

Their lovemaking strained the seams of her sleeping-bag and the air around them became stifling.
Dilke threw back a corner of the canopy and moonlight flooded in, turning his face chalk-white and
gleaming on the perspiration which beaded her skin.

'Poor old Jon!' He spoke into her neck.

'You are a *beast*.' She gave emphasis with her
knuckles in his ribs.

April 14th. Jon needed rest, and as they were ahead
of schedule they spent two days at Camp Ten.

The dead forest had a frosted, ethereal beauty like
trees in winter; they lay in the sun and looked across
it and talked idly.

'How did you come to ecology from geology, Jon?'
Dilke asked.

Butt did not speak immediately – then said harshly,
'Commerce has one motto: *take all – give nothing.*' He
dug between his feet with a tent-peg he had been
straightening. 'I worked as a surveyor for a petroleum
company for six years. I travelled a lot. It showed me

how blind business technology is. It will bankrupt the earth's resources before the century's out and destroy nature at the same time. Greed and stupidity will destroy an ecological balance which has taken God knows how long to evolve!'

He spoke with a passion which surprised them, then he turned the talk away from himself, as if embarrassed by the revelation of his strong feeling.

He asked Hyacinthe about her life before she was miniaturized — and Dilke about his reasons for becoming a micro-man.

Their answers, in combination, described the start of European miniaturization. Dilke spoke of the experiences of himself and his first companions.

'Olsen and Scott-Milne,' Butt interpolated.

Dilke glanced at him with mild surprise.

'I heard of them during my first stage of treatment,' Butt smiled, 'miniaturization already has its folklore.' His smile faded. 'I'm sorry they had to die.'

On the second day in Camp Ten Jon pottered about checking the climbing gear and sowing a crop of lichen. Lichen was plentiful lower down the tree but above fifty feet it was sparse, even on the shady side. Jon had collected handfuls of spores as they climbed and he now took a bagful down the northern curve of the branch where a litter of damp organic matter filled the trench bottoms. He scraped it up, mixed it with wood-ash and the lichen spores and pressed it all together into balls between his palms. Then he forced the balls into crevices with his heel.

*

April 16th. 'Two more days and we'll be there!'

It was three thousand millimetres to the next camp — their last before reaching The Branch.

After twelve days they climbed rhythmically and happily together as a team, Hyacinthe and Dilke now as assured in their movements as Butt. The arms and faces of the men were burnt brown by sun and wind, the weather was set fair. From a ledge on which they rested for a meal they could see beyond the bend in the river. The storm had blown down trees and washed soil into the river-bed; dammed-up water had spread for miles; light gleamed on the roof of a half-submerged trapper's hut. The scene had a desolate beauty.

To prolong their enjoyment of the sunshine they climbed in a westerly direction, then, when almost level with the branch on which they were to camp, they turned east.

Rounding the curve of the tree they saw, to their amazement, a large square shape resting in the crook of the branch, a rusted, dented metal container almost a foot high.

They walked into the gap between the tank and the tree-trunk and stared up with wonder at a pipe which connected them. Then they walked under the tank, made a camp three feet along the branch and ate supper.

Jonathan had a theory that the tank was a fungicide container — relic of an attempt to suppress the disease by injection.

After supper Dilke examined it through binoculars. Its olive-green paint had peeled, weldmarks showed along the seams, metal rings provided attachments for a carrying harness. Daylight faded and the tank became a featureless hulk. Dilke lay back and turned his glasses on the full moon, examining its mountains and craters till he was moon-blind. He shut his eyes and rubbed them until the black negative of the moon's circle was erased from his eyelids.

A breeze sighed in the dead branches. He lay and looked beyond the branch towards the Rockies.

A dancing shape twirled at the tip of the branch like a rag caught in the wind. It swooped and drifted away to the east, spreading and growing in volume.

Dilke scrambled up. 'It's the smoke!' he yelled.

Jon and Hyacinthe jumped to their feet and stared in the direction of his pointing finger.

Fourteen days before, and from nearly seventy feet below, they had seen a smoking branch which pointed to the west – now, smoke came from one pointing due east! They wasted no time in discussion but packed collecting bags and jars and a few simple analytical tools, then set off, eager to reach the branch's tip before it stopped smoking.

The journey to them was like a mile. Black shadows lay in the trenches between the ridges of the bark. After travelling slowly along them, unable to see hidden obstacles and cautiously feeling their way with their feet, they climbed up on to the moonlit ridges and walked quickly, balancing themselves with out-stretched arms.

The wind blew more strongly at their backs and the branch throbbed beneath them. The rising wind forced them down into the black trenches for shelter and they reverted to the blind man's pace with which they had started. Each time they looked up, the volume of smoke had increased and as they neared the end of the branch they heard a noise like a roaring furnace.

The branch was hollow; twelve inches from its end a hole opened into a groove which ran to the tip of the branch – like a railway tunnel opening into a deep cutting.

Hyacinthe, Mathew and Jon threw themselves down and stared over the arch into the groove.

A struggling mass of insects poured out of the tunnel, along the cutting, and into the air. Thousands upon thousands. Pushing, jostling, leaping, overflowing the sides of the channel, flying in pursuit of the hordes which had gone before.

The three tiny humans stared with dazed incomprehension, clutching the edge of the overhang with stiff fingers, stunned by the total unexpectedness of what they saw.

The rush of insect bodies and the clatter of their wings hypnotized and deafened the watchers. Showers of liquid filled the air with a haze of sour-smelling vapour.

They poured like smoke from the great pine on the ridge, twisting and shifting in the air above the dead trees, floating on the wind towards the distant living forests.

Then, without warning, the cataract ceased. Only a few creatures ran out; some to fly swiftly in pursuit, some to buzz on damaged wings towards the ground, some cripples to crawl along and topple into the abyss.

There was silence.

Dilke rolled on to his back and stared into space.

In his memory he saw the storm of glittering creatures climbing into the sky. He stood up abruptly, glanced at his transfixed and prostrate companions who still watched the silent cutting, then moved out along the top of an embankment and peered into the black hole. He scrambled down the incline and walked towards the mouth of the tunnel. Underfoot it was deep in stinking mud.

His companions joined him. No word had been spoken since they had come to the end of the branch. They stood and listened outside the tunnel, and heard only the sound of the wind.

Hyacinthe whispered, '*I can see a light.*'

Dilke shaded his eyes from the moon, then moved hesitantly into the tunnel's entrance and strained to see into the dark. They took a dozen more steps forward; Dilke thought he could see a faint glow in the distance – then he heard a low, growling, metallic sound behind him.

Hyacinthe screamed and he spun around.

The circle of moonlight which had marked the entrance to the tunnel was diminishing inexorably. It narrowed to a slit, then vanished; there was a thud and the sound of wind stopped; it was pitch black.

A spot of red appeared before Dilke's eyes. It floated upwards and grew into a soft, glowing ball. It paused – grew more brilliant – then dropped swiftly towards him. He raised a hand to ward it off.

A jarring concussion exploded in his head. A slow black wave pulsed outwards from the core of his brain, obliterating the fire which raged there.

PART FOUR

Ten

Dilke lay on a cold, hard surface in the dark.

He lay and listened to the fitful roar and whistle of the wind. Though conscious of the horizontal surface beneath he also had a sensation of floating and dipping to the left, to the left, always to the left, as if his body was unsupported there. He turned his head away to correct the balance and a storm of lights like sparks from a forge struck him behind the eyes. The burning was so intense that he dared not cry out for fear of increasing and prolonging it. He kept his head rigid and slowly the pain died.

A line appeared between the slits of his eyelids. He considered it for a while: it trembled and shimmered like a band of white light seen through water.

Was he underwater?

Slowly he opened his eyes. A smooth bank of snow lay before him; the tops of two bell-tents appeared above it. Beyond them a white landscape extended to infinity, ridged and rucked by the wind. The yellow sun flared above and dazzled his half-open eyes.

He knew instinctively who was in the dark tents: Hyacinthe and Jonathan in one and Bill Olsen and Henry Scott-Milne in the other. He must go to them; but something held him fast along his left side. Cold as ice. A snowdrift?

To the right, on the soft perimeter of his vision, he could see the base of a great ice cliff. He moved his head to examine it and the pain spun again in the sockets of his eyes, a burning snowstorm driving across the landscape.

He brought up his hands to cover his eyes.

The tent on the right lifted into the air and meta-morphosed into a hand which floated over the snow-ridge towards him, then hung before him, trembling slightly. He was so astonished that – impervious to the pain it caused – he raised his head to examine it more carefully.

It was his own hand, streaked with dirt. He looked beyond it and willed the remaining tent to move but it stayed motionless; under his intense gaze the conical shape changed into the knuckles of his closed and partially concealed left hand. He sent back his right hand to raise it; the lifted hand was cold and limp and when pressed between fingers and thumb was without sensation. He dropped both hands into the snow and laid back his head and closed his eyes to concentrate on this visual riddle.

Beneath his hand the snow was not cold; he rubbed his fingers lightly to and fro and felt a coarse and rather stiff texture which yielded when he slid his arm to the right. His hand came to the cliff and climbed it; it was cold, but not icy, with a surface like rough plaster.

Dilke opened his eyes fully, stared at the whiteness below and saw the criss-crossed fibres of a canvas sheet; after long examination of its warp and weft he brought his hand from the wall and tentatively raised the edge of the sheet. His body lay beneath it, revealed by the soft light which filtered through the material. His chest rose and fell irregularly, the wind whistled and growled in his throat and he hawked up phlegm from his congested lungs and swallowed it;

114

it had a bitter and acidic taste. His vest was clean but, as he raised the sheet higher, he saw that his trousered legs were caked with filth. A strangely familiar, yet elusive, odour billowed from under the sheet as he lowered it. He closed his eyes to hide from the glare and frowned with the effort to discover the associations of the smell.

The memory came at last – a flash in the darkness of his head.

The red explosion across the black and (reversed in order) the floating light, the entry into the tunnel, the heavy odour and the winged insects pouring from the tip of the hollow branch.

Contented with the recovery of these visions, he lay without movement for some minutes, then he reached up to scratch an itch on his right cheek and felt a streak of dry, crystalline substance down the side of his face. He followed it up to his forehead where he found a break in the skin and grunted with pain when his fingers touched the raw, wet flesh.

He examined his fingertips: the liquid, clear and slippery, was not blood.

He resumed the exploration. The wound was like a star, high on the right side of his forehead, breaking into the hairline. Some hairs were detached from his scalp and adhered to the raw surface. He picked them off gingerly, a few at a time, and examined them minutely until he became bored with the occupation. But now he was alert.

The place was like a crude cellar, without defined corners and with a curved ceiling from which hung a bare bulb. Its whitewashed surfaces were roughly grooved like a cave chiselled out of ice.

He cleared his throat, which precipitated a fit of

coughing. The cold struck into his back. Jesus! it was cold. He had to get out of here. He turned his head and saw an irregular doorway closed by a metal door. He pulled the cover aside, pushed with his right hand and sat up swaying. He started to swing his legs round to the floor but his feet caught in the sheet, his left arm dropped loosely over the edge of the bench and he toppled over in a great arc. He lay, half stunned, in a grotesque attitude, one side of his face pressed against the floor, his legs bent back, his feet still trapped in the sheet.

The floor was a deep honey colour, as smooth and as cold as glass, marbled with dark flecks and lines beneath its translucent surface. He coughed weakly and an oyster of phlegm slid on to the shining surface; he sighed wearily and watched it slowly spread.

The door screeched open and feet marched across the floor. Two steel-shod clogs stopped a fraction away from his eyes and then he was grabbed under the armpits and flung back on to the bench. The micro-man who stood over him was dressed in black leather. The zipped tunic, open down the front, showed white skin; the skin on his hands and scowling face was also pure white and his hair was cropped to a blond stubble. A Black-and-White man, thought Dilke dreamily.

'What is going on here?' a voice shouted.

The black-and-white man spun round and stepped away from the bench and an older man with a gaunt body and a deeply-lined face hurried into the room and glared down at Dilke. 'What is going on?' he shouted again at the man.

'It is the prisoner, Comrade Governor,' the man offered.

'It is the prisoner!' shouted the old man. 'Get the doctor! Get the doctor!'

'And bring a stretcher!' he called after the running man. He pulled up the sheet to Dilke's chin, then folded his arms tightly across his chest and rocked impatiently from side to side. 'Hurry up! Hurry up!' he muttered. He had a bold nose, eyes set deep beneath thickets of white eyebrows and a mane of white hair.

A burly, stiffly-built man appeared suddenly at his side and the governor turned furiously on him. 'What is this, Kubric? Is this your business? Where *is* the doctor?' he demanded.

The man wore a crumpled grey suit; he pushed his hands into his trouser pockets, moved one foot forward and leaned over to glance coolly into Dilke's face. His shaven head was as solid as a turnip, with small oval eyes, a short, blunt nose and a tight mouth. Features which scarcely marked the smooth contours of the face. Dilke was left with an impression of white flesh, pale ginger eyebrows, flecks of blood in the eggwhite eyeballs and thin mauve lips.

The man turned squarely to his questioner. 'He'll be all right,' he said evenly.

'The man is in shock!'

'He is a spy, Comrade Governor Gravshenko.'

Gravshenko raised his shaking fists to shoulder height.

'Are we *barbarians*, Kubric?' He ripped the sheet from Dilke's body and pointed at the bench. 'He has been lying on cold metal for twelve hours, Kubric,' he whispered savagely.

Kubric removed a hand from his pocket and leaned

forward to flip the cover over Dilke; the sheet flew up and covered Dilke's face.

When Gravshenko snatched back the sheet Kubric had gone.

Dilke heard hurried steps in the distance. A man in a white coat came in, followed by two men with a canvas stretcher.

The doctor sat on the side of the bench and tilted Dilke's head to examine the wound then took out a watch and laid his fingers on the artery in Dilke's neck. There was a long silence.

'Mmm.' The doctor rose abruptly, threw the crumpled sheet into a corner and nodded the stretcher-men forward.

Dilke sagged in their grasp; the quick lift from bench to stretcher made his head spin. The ceiling bulb danced and oscillated, evolving coiling, twisting aerial patterns, inducing a feeling of nausea. He shut his eyes and lurched into blackness, rolling over and over like a corpse in water.

He was floating again in the dark. The sensations of the moment blurred into the past; the snow, the tent-into-hand mutation, the cliff of ice, the white cave, the hostile, outraged, indifferent, impassive faces – all had the same hallucinatory quality. Now the shuffle and scrape of feet died and silence returned.

'Mathew?'

He reopened his eyes. He was still in the presence of the white-faced men but two others now stood amongst them. Hyacinthe gazed tearfully down at him and Jonathan Butt stood beside her.

'Halagalal,' he mumbled. He tried again to say her

name, 'Hala–Hagalacin.' His tongue clucked loosely in his mouth. Hyacinthe knelt beside the stretcher and caught up his hand and pressed it against the side of her face.

The governor stooped and patted her gently on the shoulder. 'He will be all right, he will be all right,' he said in English: it was both a gesture of comfort and a sign that Dilke must go.

Dilke considered the words carefully as if they had a special significance – shadowy, secondary, yet profoundly important. Behind the commonplace words hung an abstract meaning which he was too tired to grasp – was it the repetition of the phrase which gave it an extra dimension?

His eyes, now blurred with fatigue, moved towards the old man's face. Understanding came slowly ... these were the first English words the man had spoken. Dilke looked at the other white faces ... all previous words had been Russian ... he had translated subconsciously. He smiled to himself, pleased with the thought, as if he had contrived a secret victory.

Hyacinthe squeezed his hand more tightly, he could feel her trembling fingers linked with his own. The hand which had been insensible to feeling now felt the wet tears on her cheek. The yielding canvas was soft and warm beneath him. Dilke closed his eyes again.

Eleven

Mathew Dilke awoke in a hospital ward which had the same rough walls and ceiling as the cell from which he had come.

The light was dim. He counted twelve beds. A crop-headed, white-skinned man slept in the next bed; the others were empty. The man had a face like a Turk, with deep-set eyes, an aquiline nose, a bitter mouth and a sweeping white moustache which curved down on each side of his heavy jaw.

Dilke recalled, with great clarity, his experiences since entering the hollow branch. Now he examined his physical condition.

His lungs were clear; a bandage encircled his head; his left hand, though stiff, was warm and sensitive to touch. The fingers and thumb were clenched together into the palm, he pulled them straight with his good hand and massaged them until they were relaxed and he could move them voluntarily.

The sound of footsteps came from a door at the end of the ward and the lights grew brighter. The white-coated medical orderly who had helped to lift him on to the stretcher walked in. He spoke in Russian to Dilke's neighbour. 'Good morning, Grishka Kazakov.' Then with raised voice he called to the empty beds on the other side of the ward, 'Good morning, Comrade Petronovitch!'

A head slowly rose from between two beds and glared at him.

Without quite knowing why he did so, Dilke feigned

sleep. He watched through his eyelashes; the orderly examined a chart at the end of his bed and asked, 'Has he moved in the night?' Dilke's neighbour grunted non-committally.

After looking thoughtfully at the motionless Dilke the man left the ward – then returned with breakfast for the other patients.

Dilke covertly watched the man in the next bed as he ate, and listened to the clink of spoon on bowl from the other patient's hiding-place.

Dilke discovered that he was ravenous.

He gave up his pretended sleep and stirred on his bed, gave an abbreviated groan, blinked repeatedly and stared at the ceiling.

The orderly appeared at his bedside, leaned over and said, 'How are you?' in Russian.

'Where am I?' Dilke said in English.

'Do you understand Russian?' The man again spoke in Russian.

Dilke stared at him vacantly and the man left and brought food and fed him with a spoon.

The orderly cleaned the ward after breakfast, making Petronovitch return his mattress from the floor to a bed. The man sat on the bed, staring with extraordinary concentration at the floor, his brows forced together and his mouth moving soundlessly, as if working out a problem of great complexity.

After the departure of the orderly with his broom Petronovitch turned his face to the wall and with sudden passion shouted, 'Leave me alone!'

Though Dilke's thoughts were lucid he was tired and he slept occasionally during the day.

Kazakov had visitors in the evening. Dilke heard the scrape and clatter of clogs in the corridor. Through half-opened eyes he watched two heavy-set men enter the ward in their bare feet and sit on each side of Kazakov's bed. They wore stained leather clothes and their shaven heads and white faces were smeared with dirt; they carried with them the smell of insects.

Dilke lay with closed eyes and listened without much interest to the conventional exchange of hospital-visit chat.

'How was he caught?' asked Kazakov. Then, as if to reassure his visitors, 'He does not speak Russian.'

Dilke was suddenly *very* interested.

'At the east gate, with two others,' one of the men said. 'Piatra Kolliarov and Maksim Atarshchikov got them three nights ago. This one got a rod on the head.'

The other man laughed and went click! click! click! with his tongue in a rising cadence. 'He must have a head like rock—he got a Three-Charge. Chief Engineer Kubric would give him Four if he had his way!'

There was a lull in the talk; then Kazakov asked, 'And how is Number Four Shaft going?' The apparently innocent question remained unanswered. Dilke sneaked a look at the men; one looked down at the bed with suppressed amusement, the other stared at Kazakov with a tight down-turned smile on his face. They said goodbye and left.

The lights were dimmed after supper.

Grishka Kazakov went to sleep quickly; Dilke listened to the soft, repeated cough of the man on the floor and wondered at the significance of the Three-Charge Rod and Number Four Shaft.

By next morning Dilke had worked out a strategy. To his pretended ignorance of the Russian language he added the pretence of a paralysed hand and a show of witless friendliness, nodding and grinning impartially at his fellow patients and the medical orderly.

It was bath-day. The orderly took away the sullen Petronovitch and Dilke heard their discordant voices above the hiss of the shower. When Petronovitch returned, Grishka Kazakov pulled off his long night-shirt and stood naked by his bed. His body, like his bony face, had a gaunt power.

Dilke stared at him in astonishment, his show of amiable lunacy forgotten for the moment.

Kazakov had only one leg; his left leg was off at mid-thigh—and his white body was covered in a fantastic pattern of tattoos.

Only his head, hands, genitals and foot were not tattooed; the rest was covered with a swirling pattern of insects picked out in blue and faded red.

Drawn in meticulous detail, a creature with widespread wings lay across his chest—Dilke recognized it clearly as the species which had flown out of the branch. More of them covered his arms and legs. Kazakov turned and moved with agility down the ward, hopping from bed to bed and steadying himself with his hands on the bed-rails.

A horde of wingless insects with fat bodies and round heads swarmed up from between his buttocks and covered his back and sides. Crouched between his shoulder-blades a six-legged monster with great toothed jaws seemed to dance and sway as he hopped towards the shower.

Dilke's left leg gave way when he got out of bed — without the orderly's support he would have fallen flat. He was assisted to the shower where he sat in the cubicle and was washed down. He was weighed in the small surgery, then left alone to await the doctor.

Dilke examined the room and its contents. A desk, a couch, a door leading to another room—perhaps an operating theatre. Next to his chair was a glass case full of medical instruments: hypodermics, catheters, dental forceps, a stethoscope, a round mirror on a headband ...

Dilke slid back the glass door and took out the mirror. His face was yellowish, the tanned skin turned pale by illness; the hair around the wound on his forehead had been cut away—and shaved completely from his head for good measure.

He heard a noise outside, quickly replaced the mirror on its glass shelf and silently closed the door. The doctor entered and motioned him to stand. Dilke stood up swaying, then leaned against the cabinet for support.

'What is wrong with your leg?' the doctor asked curtly. For a moment Dilke was disconcerted by the unexpected English words, then he swung the leg to and fro and said, 'I can't walk, Doctor.'

'Let me see you walk!'

Dilke gently put his weight on the stiff leg; it supported him, but when he moved the knee unlocked. He fell forward, grabbed at the desk then shuffled back to the chair. He grinned inanely.

The doctor put a stethoscope to his back and front, raised his eyelids with a thumb and examined each eye in turn, then he called the orderly and said in Russian, 'There is probably some brain damage but basically he is sound.'

As Dilke was helped to his bed Kazakov jigged his stump up and down beneath the bedclothes and shouted in his harsh accent, 'They are going to take off your leg, Comrade!'

Kazakov had a rough sense of humour, often shown in a mutual exchange of insults with the orderly and a rather heartless joshing of the deranged Petronovitch. Dilke permitted himself a smile – edged with a suitable lack of comprehension.

When Dilke was back in bed his neighbour took a board and a set of crude ivory chessmen from his locker and mimed an invitation to play.

Kazakov's chess was direct and brutal.

Dilke played like a novice – and though his opponent allowed him to replay his more absurd moves, it was to prolong the game in cat-and-mouse fashion. In the first game Dilke was mated in ten moves. During the second he became aware that they were being watched. Petronovitch had crept up silently and was staring at the board with his habitual expression of tortured concentration; his brows worked up and down and his lips pursed and pouted, emitting a jumble of sighs and indecipherable words.

Suddenly he dashed up his hand beneath the edge of the board, scattering the pieces, and shouted petulantly, 'Leave me alone!' and rushed to his bed in the corner.

'Porca miseria!' swore the Russian. He called the orderly. 'It is time for his happy-pills, do you not think, Comrade?' he said as the man retrieved chessmen from under the beds.

The Italian expression of abuse coming from the Russian's mouth surprised Dilke; he leaned forward and said earnestly, 'Capisce Italiano?'

Kazakov fell back against his pillows and spread his hands in an Italianate gesture of affirmation.

Until now Dilke's information had come from eavesdropping; by using this shared language he could now learn more from the Russian – without destroying his cover.

In answer to Kazakov's questions he told him the truth, more or less: that he was employed by the Canadian government to investigate the tree disease (hoping that neither Jon nor Hyacinthe had revealed his connections with Whitehall and micro-training).

Kazakov had learned his Italian swearing in Italian engineering camps. 'The Italians are the best road-builders and dam-builders in the world – next to we Russians!'

The Russian needed no encouragement to talk about himself. He was of Dilke's age; a Georgian ('like Stalin!' he boasted); a foreman engineer and electrician ...

Dilke brought the talk round to other people. To Petronovitch, the orderly, the doctor; to the governor and Kubric.

'Deputy Governor Kubric! *There* is an engineer,' Kazakov shouted. 'What a bastard!' he added admiringly.

'How long have you known him?' asked Dilke.

'For *five* years, Comrade. But soon we shall go home. Five years is enough! We signed for only four. Five years is too long. You see the results ...' Kazakov rapped his temple with a forefinger, then pointed at Petronovitch who sat on the far bed with the orderly standing over him holding a glass of milky fluid.

'Petronovitch *was* all right; he worked in the Nest till his nerves went. You get tired, and then you get careless, and then ...' he slapped the stub of his thigh '... and then you get this! A little soldier took it ...' Kazakov stiffened his forearms and his flattened hands then scissored his arms across each other like blades.

The Russian leaned forward and said hoarsely, 'And now I will be an old man. All Georgians live to be old. I will live to be a hundred and fifty years old. Perhaps more!'

They replaced the chessmen and started their game again. As they played, Dilke attempted to frame questions which would be searching and yet seem guileless.

Kazakov was taking longer over his moves and Dilke saw, with a small jolt of realization, that his own recent moves had been preparation for an attack on his opponent's inadequately developed position.

It was not too late to save the situation: he brought his queen to the centre of the board and it was briskly taken by a knight. Kazakov did not offer to return the piece.

Petronovitch joined them and sat tranquilly on the edge of Kazakov's bed and watched the play. Dilke's game collapsed satisfactorily after the loss of his queen.

They re-set the board. Petronovitch who had been dreamily examining and fondling the sacrificial queen obediently placed it in Kazakov's outstretched hand.

'He is happy now,' said Kazakov in Italian.

'You are happy now?' he said to the smiling Petronovitch. 'There are no more termites under the beds.'

Kazakov said to Dilke, 'He sleeps on the floor

because he is afraid the termites will grab him as he gets into bed!' He laughed. 'He lies on the floor so that he can watch out for them!'

Kazakov turned again to Petronovitch and ordered, 'Show the comrade your legs.'

The man raised his coarse dressing-gown to mid-calf and Kazakov roughly pulled it up over his knees. The legs were coloured brown and pink and yellow – like cooked meat in aspic. At first Dilke thought that they were tattooed then saw that it was eczema.

'Touch them!' said Kazakov. 'Go on, they are quite dry.'

Dilke touched the apparently raw flesh and found it to be dry and scaly. Petronovitch quietly pulled down his clothes.

Kazakov said to Dilke, 'He is psychotic. He thinks the termites will take us over. It has gone to his brain – and it has come out like that on his legs.'

Petronovitch sat on the bed and smiled serenely.

Grishka Kazakov was sated with victory; he gave Petronovitch two knights to play with and then put the board away.

Petronovitch held up the little horses and brought their ivory noses together. He saw Dilke's eyes upon him and raised the pieces higher, tapped them gently together and laughed softly.

Dilke lay awake thinking.

The climb to the source of the 'smoke' had led to discovery of this extraordinary community.

A society provided with advanced medical facilities ... engaged in micro-engineering ... a clandestine project (the man Kubric had called Dilke a spy) of some magnitude, now in its fifth year ... concerned in some way with flying termites ...

The facts fitted together like crazy-paving but led nowhere.

Why were the Russians here?

Members of an alien country living within a Canadian tree.

Instinctively, Dilke felt that there must be significance in their presence at the heart of the blighted forest.

He turned restlessly on his bed. If only he could see Hyacinthe and Jonathan – *they* might have discovered something.

Twelve

At breakfast-time Dilke asked the orderly – with proper deference – if he could see his companions and in the afternoon two guards brought them to his bedside.

Hyacinthe's eyes were puffed with weeping and a fading bruise marked the side of Butt's face.

In front of Kazakov Dilke kept up an appearance of semi-paralysis and under the eyes of their guards his visitors were tense and constrained. They exchanged no more than platitudes before the girl and the man were taken away.

Though the visit was short and unsatisfactory, it brought Dilke's thoughts into focus.

They were prisoners and somehow they must escape – when he knew why the Russians were there!

First he must leave the ward and join his companions.

That night while the Russians slept Dilke worked on his leg; massaging it, flexing the knee and ankle and moving the toes until the whole leg ached. He sat on his bed in the semi-darkness, then cautiously stood up; the leg shook but he was able to take a few painful steps.

The doctor saw him again next morning and seemed satisfied, even a little surprised, at his improvement, and on the following day a guard came for him.

130

Supported by the orderly, he limped along a corridor with rough white walls and ceiling like those of a tunnel hewn out of chalk. They turned off into a narrower passage with steel doors on each side. Dilke entered an open doorway and found himself in his cell once more, even the canvas sheet still lay in the corner. The orderly left bedding, and the guard closed and locked the door.

He had not made much progress; his hope that he might join Hyacinthe and Jon to plan an escape was disappointed. But at least he had a mattress and adequate bedding for the steel bench. After an interval he hammered on the cell door and indicated to the guard a need to urinate. The lavatory was just across the corridor. The guard accompanied him and sat on a wash-basin and scowled. Dilke felt that the man's ill-will was not directed at him personally but was evidence of a bleak depression which all the Russians shared – even the extrovert Kazakov's face became a bitter mask when he slept.

A special agent's function is to observe. Dilke had not lost his old skills. During his halting journey to and from the lavatory he used his eyes, and back in his cell he lay down and reviewed what he had seen:

> The guard wore grenades as sidearms; they were canisters on sticks and hung down, six-gun fashion, at each side of his belt. He carried a rod, three millimetres long, with a metal block clipped on behind the handle.
> The lavatory was extensive, with two showers, four W.C.s, four wash-basins and a row of urinals;

its outer door was open as was the door to the next room, which was piled high with cases.

Opposite was Dilke's cell door, then two other doors which were closed.

A chair stood against the wall of the main corridor giving a view into the passageway.

Dilke closed his eyes and concentrated on the memory of the three doors on his side of the passage. The two other sliding doors had been secured by single heavy bolts dropped into holes in the floor. He turned his head and examined the interior of his own door; a blue discolouration marked the bottom left corner of its rusted surface – sign of a new weld. The cell was clearly makeshift, but though its crude bolt could easily be lifted from outside it could not be moved from within.

There were still things he could do. He could exercise – unobserved, as the door was without a window or a peephole – and he could listen.

Between punishing bouts of exercise he sat by the door with his ear to its cold surface and listened to voices and the sound of feet outside.

Thirteen

Dilke had progressed to squats by the following day. He also practised a limp for use outside his cell.

He was stepping up and down on to the bench to counts of a hundred when the bolt was drawn and the guard appeared at the door. Dilke limped into the passage with his left arm thrust inside his shirt and found a second Russian guarding Hyacinthe and Jonathan. He grinned with pleasure and squeezed the girl's hand. They were marched along corridors and up stairs, and a guard threw open double doors. They entered a large room, their eyes dazzled by ceiling lights; the place seemed to be full of men.

Governor Gravshenko rose from the head of a long dinner-table and waved them forward. He said in slow and carefully enunciated English, 'Please, will you come in?' Then he turned and looked around and smiled, 'Comrades, I wish you to meet our intruders!'

The Russians regarded them with curiosity.

Gravshenko indicated each man in turn: 'Please, will you meet Ivan Zikov. Stepan Shamil. Eugene Kornilov. Feodor Uriupin. Miron Bodovskov. Doctor Eugene Makhov. Alexis Pavlov – my assistant.' Dilke recognized only Gravshenko and the doctor.

They sat near the head of the table next to the old man's assistant, first Dilke, then Hyacinthe, then Butt.

Gravshenko struck the table, making the cutlery dance. 'Where is *Kubric*?'

He paused, dismissed the subject with a wave of his hand and turned to his neighbour. 'Pavlov! Kindly bring soup for our guests.' Pavlov was short, plump, obedient; a man of about twenty-four with a round forehead and protruding top teeth.

'Doctor Makhov considers that your health has much improved.' Gravshenko smiled at Dilke and raised a glass. 'I drink to your good health, and please permit me to say, I regret that you all must suffer confinement while we are here.'

Dilke raised a glass in reply; it contained a clear spirit of considerable potency.

To the would-be escaper's classic virtues of patience, watchfulness and perfidy Dilke had added kleptomania. Concealed in his mattress were such disparate and potentially useful things as a rolled bandage and a ball-point from the hospital and sheets of toilet paper and a slip of soap from the lavatory.

He slid his empty glass across the table, held it for a moment in his lap, then slipped it up under his arm (which still rested, as if in a sling, within his un-buttoned shirt) and grasped it through the shirt fabric with his left hand. It would make an effective resonator, enabling him to hear more clearly through his cell door.

They had progressed to the main course when Kubric entered, carried his food from a hot-plate on the side-table and sat down at the only vacant space, opposite Hyacinthe.

His presence brought silence to the table. He ate — looking neither to the right nor left — as if he were alone.

Gravshenko stared down the room and said loudly in Russian, with a note of petulance, 'Eight o'clock is dinner-time!'

Kubric washed down a mouthful of food with water and quietly belched.

Hyacinthe cut up Dilke's meat and he ate it with a spoon. The single grey vegetable was quite without flavour.

Governor Gravshenko raised his glass high.

'Comrades! We shall drink to the Soviet Union.'

There was a respectful response from the Russians.

'And to the death of Monopoly Capitalism!' added Gravshenko. He leaned towards Dilke and smiled. 'But please understand, my friend, Krushchev's *We will bury you!* was a figure of speech – the Bomb has put the Red Army out of business. And, besides, capitalism contains the seeds of self-destruction within itself.'

Gravshenko leaned back and addressed the room.

'*Our* society rests, like a great pyramid, secure on the broad base of the people's approval. The capitalist pyramid is upside down, balanced on the profit motive – where a capitalist's heart should be he keeps a profit motive!'

The Russians laughed dutifully.

Dilke nodded agreeably.

Kubric kept his eyes on his plate.

'A little *push* ... ', Gravshenko poked out a bony finger, ' ... and the capitalist pyramid will fall. Then they will have anarchy, leading to chaos, followed inevitably by the rise of a People's Democracy. The spread of communist ideals in the factories and fields of the West is hurrying forward the day of revolution, and the sabotage of capitalist resources is fast weakening its economy.' The old man glanced ironically at his guests. 'Sabotage is not just placing dynamite under railway engines … '

Kubric got up abruptly and walked out.

Gravshenko faltered, glared at his deputy's retreating back, then refilled his glass and drank moodily. The room was hushed. Dilke deftly pocketed his spoon: a possible excavator with which to undermine the bolt on his cell door.

Gravshenko began again more quietly, speaking almost to himself. 'The superiority of our technology over capitalist technology is unquestionable … even our sabotage is a synthesis of mechanics and microbiology … but still there are lessons to be learned. Our thinking is not static. We move forward towards an ideal socialism … '

He looked towards his three guests and smiled. 'There is a race of great antiquity which invented civilization three hundred million years before man was born. Its society is more ancient, more complex and more stable than even those of ants and bees. Its environmental control is total; its social organization is unsurpassed; compared to it, man is in his social kindergarten!

'"Man has a lofty understanding, but for the most part it is vain and false. That of brute creation is less, but it is utilitarian and exact. And a small certitude is preferable to a vast delusion."'

Gravshenko smiled again. 'In that passage da Vinci could have been describing the termite – as a social engineer the termite is certainly utilitarian and exact. And yet the word *brute* does not suggest the essentially moral quality of termite life – in which the virtues of discipline, duty, love and individual self-sacrifice are paramount.'

Suddenly Gravshenko emptied his glass and rose impulsively to his feet.

'Come with me!' he said.

He left the dining-chamber, taking with him his guests and the man Pavlov, followed by the guards. He went before them down a corridor and entered an unlit room. Sweeping his hand down a panel of switches he illuminated an extensive laboratory with a blaze of light and walked purposefully between long benches to the end of the room.

Pinned to the end wall were large, schematic drawings of insects. Gravshenko stopped before them, gazed at them for a moment, then turned to his followers.

'See how different in appearance are these four creatures? And yet they are of the same race, born of the same parents – were even indistinguishable one from another in their infancy.'

The drawings showed insects which were indeed very different in appearance.

The first had a neat, round head from which sprouted – like strung pearls – two delicate antennae; its body was smooth, shining and creamy-white. Gravshenko gestured towards it. 'This is a worker termite; one of the labour force which excavates the nest in which the colony lives.' Dilke and his companions saw at once that it resembled the dead creature which they had found weeks before in Bellamy's valley.

'And *here* is a soldier termite.' Gravshenko had moved to the second drawing which showed an insect comparable in size to the worker but with heavier jaws and mandibles and a head encased in armour.

The old man struck the third drawing with a bony fist. 'The warrior! Defender of the queen and her walled city.' The beast was like the soldier but much larger. Massive, heavily armoured, with huge-toothed pincers jutting from a grotesque black head.

Gravshenko smiled upon the fourth insect; a slender, multicoloured creature, with gauzy wings folded to its sides. 'And on this beautiful one depends the future of the race, for she is a sexually-mature reproductive.

'You see how perfectly each termite is fitted for its role, with the tools of its trade incorporated into its own body? Form and function are one! Each insect is part of a society of specialists with a caste system more rigorous – but less divisive – than any which has been evolved by man; and each one is endowed with a moral sense which ensures that it gives lifelong service to its community.

'Unlike human knowledge, which is recorded in ephemeral, printed form, termite knowledge is held deep within its racial memory bank.

'A termite needs no schooling, it inherits its knowledge: the worker its engineering skills and its compulsion to labour perpetually; the soldier and the warrior their martial instincts and their valour; the reproductive its irresistible urge to fly from its home and start a new colony ... ', Gravshenko paused, ' ... for a termite colony is founded by a single reproductive queen and her king.

'When atmospheric conditions are appropriate, re-productives of both sexes leave the territory in which they were born. Predators feast on the thousands

138

which fly out and only a few pairs survive to discard their wings and burrow into wood or soil and start families. At first the queen is slim and active, mother of a small brood, but as her family grows they take over the care of the nest, leaving her to grow fat and give birth. After helping to found the colony and care for his firstborn, the king's remaining duty is to refertilize his wife at intervals. This he faithfully does for the rest of his life—a long one by insect standards, as he may live for ten years.'

There was a fifth drawing. A sectional drawing of an extensive and immensely complex system of chambers and passageways.

Gravshenko rubbed his dry hands together with enthusiasm. 'The city state! A miracle of civil engineering!' His finger danced over the surface of the drawing, indicating dormitories, nurseries, barracks and the traffic lanes which linked them together—and to a chamber at the base of the vast labyrinth on which the old man's finger came to rest. 'Here, central to the life of the whole community, is where the queen lies in perpetual labour, adding to the population by night and day.

'And what *sustains* her enormous family?' Gravshenko looked interrogatively at his mute audience.

'They feed on the very substance from which their home is made! A material which constitutes the greater part of all trees. *Cellulose*, the most common and least digestible vegetable substance in the world.

'How does the termite digest this stubbornly indigestible material?'

Again Gravshenko answered his own question. 'The termite is only the visible half of an extraordinary symbiotic partnership. In its hind gut swarm vast numbers of benign parasites, protozoa which digest the fragments of wood and return them as sugar to the host insect ... '

Gravshenko reached out, took a glass jar from a shelf full of jars and unscrewed its lid. Floating in a clear liquid were small creatures like bottled mussels, coloured blue-black and cream-white, fringed with whiskers at one end. He transferred one of them to a bench-top; there was a pungent odour of formalin; he pressed the dead creature and fluid oozed from it on to the bench. 'The existence of the whole territory depends on these small creatures. Deprived of protozoa the termite dies of starvation even though it may gorge itself to bursting-point.'

They watched him poke at the liquid with his forefinger, pushing small fragments of wood to the edge of the pool. Then – as if their silence implied scepticism – he looked up sharply and said irritably, 'I have proved it experimentally!'

'Fascinating,' exclaimed Dilke, who had abandoned his show of mild imbecility. 'You are the discoverer of some extraordinary mysteries, Governor Gravshenko.'

Gravshenko smiled.

'Yes. My researches have been unquestionably successful. The functioning of the termite and its caste system is no longer a mystery.'

He extended a hand to the line of drawn insects. 'First, remember that an infant termite can become a member of any of the four castes – and then realize that a proper numerical balance must be kept between the caste members ...

'Now. Answer this question: how does the termite community influence the infant's choice of caste?'

The old man looked brightly from face to face and they awaited his inevitable answer to the riddle.

'My research has shown that each termite caste has its own chemical trademark and the relative amounts of these chemicals within the nest reflect the relative strength of the four castes. The immature termite's choice of vocation is influenced by this chemical mixture. If, for example, the soldier chemical is too strong it means that the army is too big and the young termite looks elsewhere for an occupation – in effect the termite is recruited into the weakest caste, where it is most needed.

'A question remains: we know that a young termite understands a chemical language – but with which organ does it perceive it?'

Gravshenko tapped his midriff.

'With its stomach! Food-exchange goes on ceaselessly between all termites, and infant termites receive their chemical messages mixed with the predigested stomach contents of their elders.'

Behind the governor's back Pavlov smothered a yawn. The monologue was over. But there was still a postscript. Gravshenko's expression changed, complacency was touched with exultation; his eyes glittered beneath his frosted eyebrows.

'I have mastered the termite language! Synthetic chemical trademarks have been formulated in this laboratory. When our food-exchange researches are complete I will regulate the caste system as I choose.

'Come to my office. I will show you the figures on food-exchange.'

He preceded them up a flight of open stairs at the end of the laboratory and took them through a door. In the centre of the room a desk stood in a pool of light.

Gravshenko bent his head to search a drawer and his mane of hair fell apart, revealing a bare patch of skin mottled brown, pink and yellow. Petronovitch's skin complaint! Manifestation of an inner discord. Gravshenko scrabbled in drawer after drawer.

'*Look* for them, Pavlov.' His assistant, having cleaned up the protozoa and its pickling fluid now joined the search.

A light caught Dilke's eye.

Above Gravshenko's head the moon shone brightly.

Dilke stared incredulously. Then, turning on his heel, he realized that they had entered an observation chamber. The room was perfectly circular and through its huge windows he could see not only the moon but moonlit valleys on all sides of the tree.

From this room! Through the glass! A way of escape!

The guards had remained below in the laboratory.

Dilke's heart began a heavy beat.

Gravshenko's voice interrupted his flying thoughts. 'You admire the view from my camera obscura?'

Dilke did not understand.

Gravshenko pointed upwards. 'It gives me three-hundred-and-sixty-degree vision. From here I can see a hundred miles to every compass point!'

Dilke looked up.

A massive stainless-steel tube pierced the ceiling and hung above the governor's desk. In its base, like that of a submarine periscope, was a cluster of lenses. A thin track of light joined the moon to one of them.

The moon was a projected image; the windows a a smooth white wall. The escape route was a mirage.

Dilke forced a strained smile of appreciation for Gravshenko's moonlight view.

On a panel beneath the lenses were five dials:

Ве́тер направля́ть. Ско́рость. Темлература.
Вла́жый. Воздух давле́ние.

Wind and weather information.

This was something new.

How could he switch Gravshenko from the trivia
of termite gastronomy to the subject of meteorology?

But the old man had returned to his search. From
the papers piled on his desk he snatched up a sheet
with an exclamation of pleasure. It was a micro-
copied photograph of an arid sunlit plain with a tall,
spongelike structure in the foreground. On one side a
Negro stood, holding a bucket. On the other side
stood Gravshenko before miniaturization — a young
Schweitzer in shorts, white plimsolls and a domed
sun-helmet.

'When I was studying the terrestrial termite in
Africa I poured liquid concrete into a territory and
when it hardened I removed every particle of the
original structure ... '

Pavlov's face showed that he was not unfamiliar
with the story.

'It has some beauty, I think. Like a work of art ...
a piece of sculpture perhaps? But comparison with a
lung provides a better analogy; see how these branch-
ing ridges and complex passageways resemble the
bronchia. And the resemblance is more than super-
ficial. As well as being a dwelling for termites, a
territory is an organ of respiration. The air circulating
within it is continuously replenished through apertures in its outer walls.' Gravshenko circled a finger
in the air.

Pavlov found the missing file and Gravshenko put

aside his photograph to give an interpretation of the research figures.

To Dilke and Hyacinthe the figures were incomprehensible, but they aroused in Jon an interest which encouraged the governor to go ever more deeply into their significance.

The ghost of a cloud erased the image of the moon, and the panorama of dead trees and shadowed valleys dissolved from the smooth wall of the chamber. Dilke's attention wandered to the dials overhead. Wind velocity read 7 mph, direction NNE. Temperature: 4° C. Humidity: 27%. Rainfall since 1200 hrs: nil.

Dilke reached out stealthily for Hyacinthe's hand. Her eyes remained fixed on the papers which littered the top of the desk but she gently returned the pressure of his fingers.

Butt (whose wooden silence in the dining-room and laboratory had not helped Dilke's efforts to harmonize East/West relations) had progressed from occasional grunts expressing interest to inquiries about margins of statistical error and methods of sampling.

'We have taken our samples from the upper termitory, but when Pavlov has fed radio-isotopes into the main colony the final research stage will begin.'

Gravshenko stuffed the papers and graphs back into a folder and with a peremptory 'Come with me, I will show you the termitory', he hustled them from the room and through the laboratory.

Dilke went with a new expectancy: within the termitory might lie the clue to its purpose! To keep up with the old man he moderated his apparent disability, limping doggedly along corridors and retaining a more spectacular crippled gait for the descent of stairs.

Fourteen

The corridor opened into a vast cavern almost twelve inches long with a high, arched roof nearly lost in shadow.

A metal cat-walk, lit by a row of overhead lights and elevated above the uneven floor on a criss-cross of girders, stretched down the length of the cave.

They clattered after Gravshenko on to the walk. Below them in the floor of the cavern there was a well filled to the brim with green liquid. Dilke and his companions paused to look down; banks of foam lay on the sluggishly moving fluid; a sour smell of fermentation rose to their nostrils. They hurried after the old man, who had bustled on ahead, and crossed two more wells which contained clear water. At the end of the cavern a fourth well was being excavated. Two engineers stood on the cat-walk, looking down into the wide pit.

'This is Number Four Shaft which will supply more water to the main territory.' Gravshenko and his party leaned over the handrail and looked down.

A fluctuating red light glowed deep in the shaft's interior. Ninety millimetres below, a winking red bulb suspended on a length of cable dimly lit five worker termites lying in excrement on the shaft bottom — like white pigs in a circular sty.

Four of them chewed weakly at the floor of the pit each time the bulb glowed. The fifth insect lay still.

Gravshenko spoke to an engineer. The man pressed two buttons on a control panel; the red light went out and a spotlight shone down. He pushed a lever; an electric winch hummed in the darkness above their heads and a big steel hook came down on the end of a cable and stopped level with the cat-walk. The second man climbed over the rail and steadied the swinging cable; he put a foot in the curve of the hook and stood up on it. His comrade pushed the lever and he sank to the pit bottom and hung just above a termite. He slid a rod from his belt. Four sharp clicks in succession, like the sound of a ratchet, came up the shaft and the end of the rod glowed red. The motionless termite was reactivated by the light into a spasm of activity; the man reached down and touched it.

There was a sharp crack and a star-shaped split opened the armoured head of the insect.

Its executioner stepped down into the muck, swung the point of the hook up under the beast's chin, then stood back and whistled.

The dead termite was rapidly winched up, swung across the catwalk and lowered on to a wide chute. The man at the control panel stretched an arm through the rails and jerked out the hook, the beast slid backwards down the chute on a film of insect blood and excreta, gradually gaining speed down the slope until it vanished through a black hole in the cavern floor.

With the same abruptness with which he had taken them from dining-room to laboratory to viewing chamber, Gravshenko led them away from Shaft Four.

The cat-walk ended at a heavy steel door in the wall of the cave. The governor slapped it impatiently, there was a sound of footsteps and a leather-clad man pushed the door open and revealed a passageway and more leather-clad men.

Twenty paces away a long section of the passage wall was broken down and rubble covered the floor. Gravshenko marched forward and peered through the jagged hole into darkness. He signalled to the men and a battery of lights flared on at the other side of the hole.

Gravshenko rubbed his hands. 'My experimental colony!'

Dilke and his companions saw a wide chamber with a low ceiling – so extensive that the light did not penetrate to its farthest point.

Dozens of pale termites stood transfixed by the glare, then they flung up their heads and careered into the dark; their bulk and their strength – and a menacing quality even in retreat – reminded Dilke of African buffalo.

One strange termite remained in view, spinning round and round on its six legs, moving in laborious pursuit of the vanished herd.

'A mutant!' shouted the old man in Russian. 'Capture that beast,' he called to the men in leather.

'Try surgery on its central ganglion to correct that eccentricity, Pavlov!'

He turned to his party with enthusiasm. 'I am using radium to improve the breed; mutations are increased by irradiation, we may get reproductives with an extended flying range. Unfortunately,' he added, 'most mutation is regressive. Some of our mutants lose sensitivity of touch, and our linked electric-shock/red-light conditioning process sometimes fails because of this.' He waved a hand at the jagged hole through which they looked. 'Last week a group disregarded the electric fence and broke out of the nest. The keepers had to use grenades on them.'

Dilke glanced at the glum faces of the keepers,

then back into the interior of the territory. A wire fence was erected across the hole, and strung along it at intervals were unlit red bulbs.

'What are the bulbs for?' he asked.

Gravshenko was lecturing the keepers and Pavlov answered for him. 'They are part of the termite conditioning process about which the Governor Gravshenko spoke. The wire is electrified. When a termite touches it it receives a painful shock of electrocution and the red lights flash on at the same exact moment; the insect learns to associate the light with pain. In time it fears the harmless light as much as the painful shock—a simple case of conditioned reflex.

'This induced fear of red light enables the engineers to stimulate the shaft-digging termites into continuous activity; they work to death in their efforts to escape from the pulsing light. Though most termites are blind they are sensitive to light. Their digging is directed downwards, they can attack only the floor of the shaft as they are confined within a ring of metal which sinks down with them as they eat.'

Young Pavlov gave the speech with a nervous lisp, then self-consciously drew down his lip to conceal his projecting teeth.

Gravshenko rejoined them.

The pirouetting mutant had disappeared, but dim shapes moved at the edge of distant shadows. Clusters of fungus, like vegetable stalactites, grew on the ceiling and hung almost to the floor. 'Wood mould,' said Gravshenko, 'on which the termites feed.'

'Do they not eat wood in preference?' Butt asked.

Gravshenko explained that the territory of the termites was circumscribed. To prevent them enlarging the nest and breaking into the domain of the

148

humans the termitory walls had been sprayed with a toxic solution of D.D.T. and copper naphthenate. Deprived of cellulose they turned to a diet of wood mould.

The termitory lights were doused. The evening's finale was over. To Dilke it was an anti-climax – though he had seen Russian termite farming in action, he remained ignorant of its purpose; now they were shepherded along the passage and out into the cavern.

The shaft-digging engineers were seated on the handrail. As the governor approached they stepped down on to the cat-walk and leaned over the rail.

Gravshenko glanced down as he passed over the shaft; only a single termite remained in the well, it lay without movement, unaffected by the fluctuating red light.

Gravshenko said in Russian, 'What is the hold-up?'

The men remained silent.

'Why are you not working?' Gravshenko demanded.

Each man waited for his companion to answer.

'Don't *stand* there, you insolent blockheads!' Gravshenko's good humour changed in an instant to shouting rage. He beat on the rail with clenched fists. 'Get it out! Get it out! Get new diggers in!'

The engineers jumped into action. The termite was winched up and disposed of; water was piped into the shaft; the diluted slurry of termite dung was pumped out. A stinking grey soup, it spurted from the pipe on to the chute and slid out of sight.

Gravshenko's shaking anger subsided but his tutorial manner had gone. His good-night was cursory and he left Pavlov to see Dilke and his companions to their cells.

Fifteen

When Dilke and Hyacinthe and Jonathan Butt were brought to the dining-room for the second time Gravshenko gave no speeches about the decadence of capitalism or the life-style of the termite but sat and moodily fidgeted with his dinner.

Pavlov spoke of their visit to the territory the previous night; talking earnestly about radio-isotopes and food-exchange. Dilke encouraged him with smiles and nods – and kept one eye on the old man at the head of the table.

Gravshenko moved his hands nervously: shifting cutlery; rubbing his cheeks and brow and neck; pushing up his cuffs and scratching his wrists – the skin on his forearms was flushed and scabrous – and darting glances at Kubric who ate with his usual indifference to his neighbours.

Gravshenko pushed aside his plate and stared up at the ceiling, savagely twirling the bristling white hairs in his left ear between finger and thumb.

'Pavlov! The glow-worms are hatching,' he cried in Russian. 'Why have you not seen to them?' There was a silence. All the Russians looked up at the overhead lights.

Pavlov, interrupted in mid-sentence, stammered, 'I am sorry, Comrade Governor. I will remove them immediately after dinner.'

'You should have removed them immediately *before* dinner.' The governor glared. 'I will not have their *shit* on this table!'

The coarseness of the word coming so incongruously from the old man almost caused Dilke to forget the speech was in Russian and show surprise.

Pavlov darted his eyes upwards then stared at the table. Dilke had not noticed the ceiling light before. Now he saw that it came from a dozen or so large white spheres which lay on a wide-meshed grille recessed into the ceiling. They shone with a cool and steady light. Dilke's eyes were caught by movement in a ball from which the light pulsed fitfully.

A worm-like embryo slowly curled and uncurled inside the translucent shape.

The globes were insect eggs. The shadows of less developed embryos were visible in several of them.

Gravshenko turned from Pavlov and shouted, 'Who were the men on Shaft Four last night, Kubric? I want them disciplined! What is wrong with your department?' he shrilled. 'That shaft has gone down only ten millimetres in a week.'

The face which Kubric turned towards his interrogator was expressionless but his pale eyes showed contempt.

'The men were at the end of the shift, Comrade Governor.'

It was a non-answer. Kubric sat back and folded his arms. For the first time Dilke noticed a violet discoloration round the man's puffed eyelids – the bruises of lost sleep – but beneath the fatigue lay a harsh and obdurate strength.

Gravshenko's jaws chewed spasmodically and his head turned stiffly on his neck as if pulled round by an invisible cord; then it swung slowly back until he stared blankly over his right shoulder. The doctor bent forward, put a hand on the governor's arm and murmured something in his ear. The old man swallowed a white tablet and in a little while became relaxed and calm; the low buzz of table-talk recommenced.

Hyacinthe leaned over and cut up Dilke's meat with shaking hands. She looked timidly across the table at Kubric, then quickly looked away.

Kubric gazed at her dreamily, a lurking sensuality in his eyes.

Jonathan Butt's cutlery went down with a clatter and Kubric's gaze moved smoothly from the girl's averted face to Butt's angry eyes. The Russian turned his head until he faced the Scot squarely and his eyes narrowed minutely.

Spots of colour flared on Butt's bearded cheeks.

Dilke chased a chunk of meat around his plate and spooned it on to his lap. He swore, then laughed, half rose to brush the food from his legs and Hyacinthe mopped gravy from his trousers.

The diversion broke the unwinking stare between the two men. Butt's eyes returned to his plate. Kubric picked his teeth, then left the room.

Gravshenko and the doctor left soon after.

The living egg in the ceiling fascinated Dilke and his companions. The creature which twisted and writhed within held their eyes fast.

'When will it hatch out, Comrade?' asked Dilke.

Pavlov, who had recovered his composure after Gravshenko's departure, thought the egg would hatch in a day or two. 'Glow-worms are neither worms nor fireflies – for which they are commonly mistaken.'

He gazed up at the eggs, 'they are the young of the *Lampyris noctiluca* beetle.'

In the absence of the governor, Pavlov lost his normal restraint and now he earnestly described the life-cycle of the insect.

'The females use their luminosity to attract flying males – though here, within the tree, I start propagation by artificial insemination. Laying soon follows and the eggs hatch into grubs which then change into adult beetles. At every stage the glow-worm is luminous. Before they are born the eggs shine through the skin of their mother's belly; the grubs shine with even greater brilliance; the adults are veritable beacons of light!'

Pavlov's pale features expressed satisfaction. 'We use them as auxiliary lighting to save electricity.'

Glow-worm breeding was a lowly job but Pavlov's interest in the insects was as obsessional as Gravshenko's preoccupation with termites.

Pavlov's fellow scientists were specialist entomologists, virologists, chemists and radiographers and his position as assistant to the governor put him low in the scientific hierarchy; only his glow-worms gave him an opportunity to do original work and for two years he had done clandestine research (aided by the chemist Bodovskov) on what made glow-worms glow.

While Pavlov talked with new-found animation the diners left the room one by one until only he and Dilke and his companions remained.

He rose to his feet as the guards entered and from politeness – or reluctance to lose his audience – he accompanied them to the cells.

A guard bolted in Hyacinthe and Jonathan, then stared at Pavlov who lingered at the entrance to Dilke's cell explaining the intricacies of the glow-worm's organic chemistry. The guard shrugged and went to his seat at the end of the passage.

In the store-room across the passageway an engineer broke open a case of grenades. Dilke listened to Pavlov and watched the man; he left the store with grenades hanging from between his fingers by their handles, went down the passage and turned the corner.

Dilke limped to his bunk and sat down with a grunt and a smile. Pavlov was encouraged to enter the cell; he leaned against the wall and gave a stage-by-stage account of the research which had led to his discovery of two substances in the tissues of the insects: luci-ferace, an enzyme, and luciferin, a fat. He had isolated the substances and brought them together within a flask of pure oxygen. Pavlov brought his palms to-gether in an oddly episcopal gesture, then threw them apart. And then there was light!

As if he had miscued a dramatic effect the lights in the cell and corridor fell to half-strength. A simulation of day and night was kept within the tree – at midnight the lights were dimmed and seven hours later regained full strength.

'Is that the time?' Pavlov exclaimed.

Dilke displayed a circle of white on his sunburned wrist and grinned, 'I'm afraid my watch was liberated!'

Pavlov stared.

'It sort of disappeared when I got here,' explained Dilke.

Pavlov's lips pursed with disapproval.

'The engineers are Kulaks!' he said bitterly.

'I must go now. Tomorrow I begin the final stage of the food-exchange research programme.'

He hesitated, then turned back from the door. 'You would like to see the lower termitory perhaps? The research takes place down there.'

Sixteen

The lift to the lower termitory was in a cul-de-sac not far from the cells. The shaft brimmed with water on which the lift-cage floated.

Pavlov's party watched the comatose and irradiated termite being lowered into the hold of the cage, then the hinged flaps in the floor were closed. They stepped in, the lift rocked gently and the door closed upon them. One of the guards pressed a button and a motor throbbed, the propeller in the base of the lift was engaged and they slowly sank into the turbulent water. The cage was an airtight capsule.

A vertical submarine! Dilke felt reluctant admiration for the concept.

Shoals of rising bubbles danced past the circular porthole in the door and the wall of the shaft flashed upwards as they sank with increasing speed. The descent was interminable. As they approached the bottom of the column of water the propeller laboured against the increasing buoyancy of the air-filled cage. A matching porthole in the lower lift gate came slowly into line with the one in the cage door; there was a click as they docked at the shaft bottom; a hiss of air as the lips around the two doors made a vacuum seal; the doors opened and they stepped out.

At the shadowed end of a long, low dormitory an off-duty nightworker groaned in his sleep.

An insomniac in a top bunk sang 'The Black Sea

Sun is Shining' to the ceiling in a muted, throaty tenor.

Near the dormitory entrance two chess players, watched by a small group of engineers, were lit by a shaded bulb. The tableau moved when Pavlov's party appeared in the doorway. The shaved heads turned, the eyes in the shadowed sockets of the corpse-white faces fixed on Hyacinthe.

Pavlov asked for Foreman Listnitsky. He had trouble with his 's's.

'Lithtnithky?' an engineer mocked. 'He is in the tanning shop.'

The tenor in the shadows laughed.

Pavlov ducked his head in embarrassment and left. He led the way along a corridor and looked into the tanning shop where termite belly skins, black with tanning fluid, hung in funereal lines. Listnitsky was not there.

They tried the slaughter-house where the floor ran with the gut-contents of butchered termites, and protozoa wriggled like tadpoles in the gutters. A butcher in the cold store directed them to the generating plant.

The lower territory corridors needed a coat of paint. Those in the upper territory were clean and white but the lower territory was a subterranean slum; ill-lit and dank; streaked with moisture stains.

The throb of a distant engine filled the air. They entered the shining arc of a metal tunnel which opened into a spacious chamber; between its steel walls the beat of the generator became more insistent.

Pavlov left them with the guards.

Dilke looked around at lathes and drills and welding gear which were grouped around a wide square hole in the floor. Metal panels were stacked in racks along one wall – the raw material from which the doors and cat-walks and the encircling metal ring around the shaft-digging termites were made.

Pavlov returned with an engineer who carried with him the smell of machine oil.

The elusive foreman was a grim, square-built man in his fifties who wiped his hands and sweating scalp with a rag, leaving a film of oil on his bald head.

Pavlov arranged for the irradiated termite to be transported from the lift and released into the lower termitory at midday. Listnitsky conversed with nods and grunts.

A faint echo of voices came up through the aperture in the floor; Dilke limped a few paces and looked down. Far below, in a pool of yellow light, two men wrestled a packing-case across a lower floor.

Pavlov joined him. 'This is the warehouse ... ' the young Russian turned and called to the departing Listnitsky and in a few moments the well of darkness was lit with a blaze of light. It was like the belly of a ship, with a series of galleries stacked with cases and machinery.

A hundred millimetres below them rows of shallow caskets were welded to the lower floor of the hold, each of a size to accommodate a micro-man – with a hinged three-quarter lid to leave the occupant's face uncovered.

'Transporter couches,' explained Pavlov. He pointed to the ceiling. 'The tank above has a capacity of eighteen million square millimetres.'

The chamber was filled with the smells of fuel oil and hot metal; heated, Dilke suddenly realized, by the mid-morning sun. They were in the tank which rested in the angle between branch and trunk.

Dilke's attention was fixed on the floor below; was there an exit down there? Though Pavlov had talked readily to him about many things since confiding the results of his glow-worm research, Dilke could think of no way to ask about an exit without arousing suspicion.

A voice spoke in Russian: 'Get out of here!'

Kubric stood behind them with his hooded eyes fixed on Alexis Pavlov. Pavlov stared with bewilderment.

'*Get out!*' Kubric rasped.

Pavlov did not speak but walked in a dazed way, followed by the rest, from the edge of the hold. The lights above and in all the galleries below went out in quick succession, leaving them in semi-darkness.

Though he had ordered them out Kubric barred the way into the tunnel; Pavlov stood before him as if hypnotized. Kubric pushed his face forward and spoke in a savage undertone.

'We have seventy millilitres of fuel left and you have every light in the place on!'

Dilke stood in the dark at the end of the line near a stack of wire coils. A short length would make a hook with which he might raise his cell-door bolt – but there were no short lengths. At his side was a bin full of bolts.

His companions hid him from Kubric, and the guards' eyes were fixed on the menacing figure silhouetted against the tunnel lights. Dilke slipped a bolt out of the bin and slid it across his body inside his shirt, trapping it between his left forearm and belly and holding its head in his concealed hand. It was more than a millimetre long; cold and heavy, a useful lever or club.

Kubric brushed past Pavlov and stalked into the dark interior of the tank.

Seventeen

Pavlov and his party hurried from the tank. A discordant sound, harsh and shrill, though muted by distance, filled the corridor.

The sound came on a current of hot air from an archway in the wall; Pavlov led them under the arch into darkness and as their eyes adjusted to the gloom they found that they were on a long balcony, high on the wall of a vaulted chamber. Dilke peered over the balcony edge.

On the floor below lay a monster sausage a hundred millimetres long.

The queen mother! Unbelievably gross. Pale as lard. Swollen with eggs. Her glistening skin pulsed rhythmically like a living organ removed from its body.

Her children swarmed around her, dwarfed by her enormous bulk.

The termite caste system which Gravshenko had so lucidly described enabled Dilke to recognize the different forms of life on the cavern floor.

But nothing he had heard prepared him for what he now saw.

To Dilke, this corpse-white maternal machine entombed in its humid chamber was obscene.

Its teeming offspring, surging in and out of the chamber, were charged with a ferocious dynamism which frightened and repelled him.

A sick odour filled the air.

F

Dilke raised his eyes. The roof was stained brown, like an oven encrusted with grease and burnt juices.

Dilke stared and stared at the floor. He began to detect a pattern in the movement of the pale beasts and a relationship between their activities and the discordant uproar which they made.

The adult workers poured into the royal chamber through an entrance near the queen's head, out-numbering all other castes by ten to one. The swelling of her body had lifted the queen's head and thorax off the floor and her legs rowed ineffectually at the air. The workers milled around and reared up in turn to feed her; she reached down her face to each one in turn and at each brief kiss a shining sphere of liquid sugar passed from lip to lip. Then each worker scurried off to join the jostling crowd at her rear.

A never-ending stream of gleaming white eggs issued from the monster's vagina, lubricated with secretions from her womb and linked with strings of creamy mucilage. Each egg was seized by a termite who avidly licked it clean and rushed with it through an exit in the chamber wall.

Pure white infants clustered by the chamber entrance and mingled with the workers who waited to feed the queen. These juvenile supplicants were tenderly licked then received gifts of her majesty's food. Some workers paused to crawl up her bulging flanks to drink oil which oozed from her skin.

Moving among the workers, like soldiers amongst civilians, termites with sickle-shaped mandibles darted forward and struck at laggards with their armoured heads, and everywhere they went they stirred up a more frenzied activity.

Carried in on the flood of workers came winged termites with red and black bodies and golden wings. Future kings and queens; creatures which, in their tens of thousands, had been the smoke which Dilke and his comrades had climbed the tree to investigate and which had led to their internment. These aristocrats struggled out of the mob and joined their fellows, exchanged luminous glances, pirouetted and flirted their lacy wings, then rejoined the stream of egg-carrying termites and left the chamber.

An iron guard of warriors encircled the queen.

Nightmare creatures, with plated black heads almost half their total length, armed with huge saw-toothed pincers.

Dilke shaded his eyes against a blaze of light which appeared to his right. A dozen paces along the balcony a Russian perched on a stool swung a spotlight round and directed its narrow beam on to the floor.

The circle of light moved away, flickered across the backs of the throng, climbed the queen's flank and came to a stop on a single termite. It froze into immobility, a strip of royal skin hanging from its jaws.

From beneath the balcony two micro-men with electric rods walked into view. One carried a weapon of normal length, the other shouldered a lance twenty millimetres long.

As they approached the line of black guards the scale of the termites was revealed. The Russians were dwarfed by the creatures, which were six millimetres at the shoulder and fully twelve millimetres long.

Within a few paces of a warrior one of the men

switched on his rod; the brute rocked uneasily from side to side. The man extended the glowing end of the rod and the termite flinched. The rod lightly touched it and it bellowed and blundered into its neighbour.

The sound had an extraordinary effect.

All activity on the floor stopped.

A savage hiss filled the chamber: a threat delivered by every termite in unison.

Dilke's cropped hair bristled. The hiss seemed to come from the very walls. The sound died slowly and echoes of it came from the apertures in the chamber walls—a chorus from distant termite millions.

Then there were only the queen's soft appeals for food and the liquid sounds of generation from within her vast interior. The population explosion continued. An egg per second was expelled on to a growing pile. The brown head and shoulders of the queen's regent pushed out from beneath her.

The armed keepers strolled through the gap in the circle of warriors and the multitude of workers parted before them. The spell was broken—the nest sprang to life again with the rattle of countless feet. The strident infants begged for food; the patrolling soldiers took their sordid meals from the rectums of the workers; the transport of eggs from the chamber recommenced, and the queen's spouse—alarmed by the noise—turned and burrowed frantically into his place of concealment beneath his wife's belly.

The keepers stood below the spotlit termite, one of them raised the lance and brought its cherry-red tip down on the creature's head. It collapsed, rolled off the queen and crashed to the floor. A termite ran exploratory antennae over the body, then wrenched off a leg and carried it away. The spot faded. Before the men had returned to their post beneath the balcony the dismembered corpse had been taken into the termite food-chain.

Dilke glanced at his companions, leaning as intently as himself over the balcony edge. He turned and looked through the arch at the guards lounging in the corridor. Engineer Kubric stood just inside the archway, in the shadows at the back of the balcony, and watched Hyacinthe. His eyes moved slowly down the girl's body and trousered legs.

Mathew Dilke discovered the man's presence with a little shock of surprise and the reflective, almost dreamy expression on Kubric's face filled Dilke with uneasiness—he called to Hyacinthe and drew her a little way along the balcony as if to improve her vantage-point. Then he called to Pavlov and asked about the execution they had just witnessed.

Pavlov explained—his voice shrill above the background noise—that an attack on the queen by one of her children was not uncommon. Conditions within the nest were not natural. The tropics were the natural habitat of termites, and the freezing Canadian winters drove them from the perimeter of the nest to its centre where unnatural overcrowding led to stress. Some termites became psychopathic—unpredictable delinquents ...

Pavlov looked at his watch and spoke to the man on the searchlight; the beam clicked on.

The two keepers came out from under the balcony driving a termite before them. It staggered on legs which were unsynchronized and before it reached the ring of warriors it collapsed. One keeper heaved it up on one side and the other stuck a goad under its tail; the beast squealed and scrambled forward.

A small soldier with its head up and its antennae twirling stepped out from between two warriors.

The irradiated insect halted, swung its head in a troubled way, then stumbled backwards. The soldier darted forward and took it in the side of the neck with its razor-sharp mandibles. A second soldier ran from under a big warrior, turned the captured termite over and ripped open its pale belly.

Hyacinthe cried out.

A stream of workers surrounded the stricken beast and its assassins – there was a violent scrum which quickly broke up. The insect from the upper territory had vanished. Only the first soldier remained, running its twitching antennae over a stain on the ground where the beast had fallen.

Dilke was surprised at the speed and savagery of the attack; he gave Pavlov a half-smile: 'Your food-exchange seems to have gone astray!'

'It is of no consequence,' shrugged Pavlov, 'the isotopes are in the food-chain now, anyway. Each time it has happened that way. In twenty-four hours –', he corrected himself, ' – in almost twenty-four hours I will take the first of a series of readings. Tomorrow I take a patrol into the territory ... '

A faint sound like the beat of a distant drum filtered into the chamber.

Pavlov raised a hand, exclaimed, 'The new guard!' and leaned over the balcony.

On the floor below, a warrior tossed his great head, clashed his jaws and began to sway rhythmically to and fro. His feet remained fixed but his oscillating body quivered and trembled convulsively. This queer dance was picked up by a neighbour and passed on to the next in line.

The insistent drum-beat grew louder. Workers surged into the chamber and scattered before a long column of huge warriors identical to those which guarded the queen. They marched in file around the queen and formed an inner ring of guards.

The dance came full circle and stopped at the warrior who had started it. There was a pause. The inner ring of warriors stepped forward. The outer ring stepped back.

The retiring guards moved slowly through the crowd, bending their ponderous heads to feed from the bowels of the swarming termite proletariat.

Eighteen

A cannibal society with a shit economy!

This was Gravshenko's virtuous Brave New World!

Dilke sat in his cell and felt nausea rising at the base of his throat and he closed his eyes and pressed his palms upon them. His mind was choked with visions of the humid black hole in the heart of the tree and its teaming maggoty population.

He felt as if he were blinded, gagged and strapped tight within layer upon layer of bindings. Sealed within his cell. Buried in the great wooden block of the tree.

Dilke threw himself back on the bunk and stared at the ceiling light in an effort to escape the feeling of enclosure – but soon the bulb dwindled to a dot. The feeling of entombment was intensified.

He escaped into memories of time and space, into visions of great distance. Landscapes, seascapes, cloudscapes. Slide of waves, blaze of sky, hot gritty desert tracks. Memories of war: he remembered the El Ageila road, himself in the lead-tank, the steering wrecked by a shell; his driver driving frantically backwards and forwards to evade the following shells.

It seemed almost funny in retrospect.

He fell asleep and dreamt that he was sleeping beneath a tank. In the dream he woke to find himself crushed by its weight. Fifty tons of metal sinking into the sand, trapping him beneath it; his sleeping-bag a death-trap preventing him from digging a way out. The underside of the engine casing pressed inexorably down on the side of his face. Through the metal he could hear the whistle and peep of morse from the tank radio-intercom. He began to howl with fear.

He woke with his cheek against the cold cell wall.

As if part of his nightmare had carried over into wakefulness he could still hear the radio. But the sound was the reality which had triggered off the dream.

His teeth and jaw ached from contact with the cold wall. He rubbed sensation back into the patch of new skin on his forehead and put his ear to the wall again. The morse was distinct but far away. He extracted the tumbler from his jackdaw collection in the mattress, placed his ear to its base and cupped its open end to the wall. The makeshift bugging device effectively removed the sound barrier.

He heard the door of the radio room slide open, the sound of footsteps, the creak of a chair. The radio yowled, and morse gave way to a Canadian D.J. advertising American cornflakes with delirious *bonhomie*. Weather for the Pacific coastline followed – fine, dry, continuing warm … courtesy of Station z39.

'And now, folks, I have a request for … '

The radio abruptly switchbacked across the soundwaves – through a sea of fragmented voices and music – and stopped on a steady, even hum.

Dilke sat with his ear to the tumbler and thought of escape.

He had found no escape route. There had been no

gap through which they could squeeze between the tunnel walls and the pipe which led into the tank. And the idea of an exit from the tank itself was pure conjecture.

He had no escape plan, but was hoping for something to turn up.

At least they had not been stuck in their cells. While they had mobility there was some chance of escape – and Dilke's cultivation of young Pavlov had led to continuation of the freedom which Gravshenko's conducted tour had given them.

Dilke's dark, claustrophobic mood of the night was replaced by the rational – and chilling – belief that their imprisonment was becoming increasingly hazardous.

He felt that Kubric threatened them. And, though Gravshenko was the nominal governor of the colony, command of the engineers gave his deputy effective control.

Dilke saw that the ill-will between the two men was becoming a bitter struggle for domination. The governor's eccentric behaviour towards the prisoners was more than mere playing to the gallery by an egocentric old man – Gravshenko's extravagant courtesy towards them, and Kubric's rigorous guard on them, were acts of confrontation.

The deep hum in the tumbler was broken by the crackle of static and a metallic cough. Dilke listened intently.

'Hello Camp Three. Jacques here! The boss says he wants the top ridge cut out Thursday. We'll be over with the Cat on Friday to pull the gear out. I'll bring the mail then. Weather forecast is fine, dry and hot – so you got no excuse!'

As the hours passed Dilke's frustration increased unbearably.

His need to escape lay side by side with a desperate wish to understand the Russian connection with the destruction of the surrounding forests – for he was now convinced that Gravshenko's passing remark about sabotage must have significance.

He ceaselessly reviewed all that he had seen and heard since his capture and paced his cell from wall to wall.

Nineteen

Kubric did not turn up for dinner.

Gravshenko made no acknowledgment of his guests but sat morosely at the head of the table, eating nothing and drinking steadily until he left halfway through the meal without a word to anyone.

His departure did little to remove the air of constraint which filled the room; the Russian table-talk was desultory and, at Dilke's elbow, Pavlov picked nervously at his food in silence.

To make conversation Dilke commented on the improved illumination from the new batch of glow-worm eggs in the ceiling.

It was as if he had pressed a switch — Pavlov began an account of the life-cycle of the glow-worm which was a repetition of the one he had given two evenings before. Dilke watched him with growing curiosity as he listened to the word-for-word recapitulation. Was this forgetfulness akin to Gravshenko's mental instability and Petronovitch's psychosis? Sign of a general stress which gripped the whole colony after years of submarine-like confinement?

As the Russians finished their meals they rose from the table and left.

Pavlov's plodding recitation stopped in mid-sentence as the door closed behind the last two scientists.

There was silence. He swallowed audibly, then muttered, 'If you take me with you I can get you out of here.'

Dilke stared at him uncertainly, unsure that he had heard properly.

A blob of perspiration trickled out of the young Russian's cropped hair and ran down the side of his face. He smeared it across his pallid cheek with a nervous forefinger.

'I have information which I can give you. And I can help you to escape.' Though his voice shook the message was clear and quite explicit.

Dilke, Hyacinthe and Butt stared with burning attention at Pavlov. His eyes darted between the shut door and their intent faces; he leaned towards them. 'There is a way of escape from the lower territory. Tomorrow I take a patrol into it to check food-exchange results. If I can arrange for you to accompany the patrol you could overpower the guards … '

The catch of the dining-room door clicked, the door opened and a guard stuck his head in.

Pavlov leapt up, a wincing smile on his face, and called in Russian, 'Yes, Comrade, yes. We were about to leave at this moment!'

As before, he went with them to the cells and remained talking to Dilke after the others had been locked up. He hesitated at the cell doorway, then slid nervously in, stood just within the door and turned his head to watch the guard take his seat at the end of the passageway. Then he whispered with hoarse vehemence, 'You and your comrades must overcome the guards! Do you understand that? All I can do is distract their attention. You understand?'

Dilke nodded expressionlessly.

'In return for political refuge I could give to your government much information.'

Dilke acknowledged Pavlov's value as an informant:

'As the governor's assistant your knowledge of this colony must be extensive ... ' his intonation added a shadowy question-mark—an invitation to Pavlov to reveal the areas of his knowledge.

Yes!

Pavlov emphatically agreed: he was familiar with the whole administration; he had kept all the governor's files for the scientific and engineering departments.

The quickness with which Pavlov recognized the veiled inquiry and his eagerness to answer it encouraged Dilke to be more specific.

How was the colony established?

How had the dual communities of man and termite been set up?

And—most vital question of all—how was the sabotage actually carried out?

Pavlov's answers came in a strained undertone, with frequent glances towards the distant guard. As the minutes passed his agitation increased. At last he burst out, 'I cannot stay! I must go now!'

'Wait!'

Dilke caught his arm and growled, 'I must talk to my companions. You must arrange it before we try an escape.'

'Yes! Yes! I will try.' Pavlov hurried from the cell and the quick tap of his steps filled the passage, were suddenly muted as he turned into the main corridor, then faded into the distance.

Escape and information in one packet!

Dilke stood in the centre of the cell, rigid with excitement, and held down a shout of joy.

All his fragmentary knowledge, his deductions and his guesswork were replaced by total comprehension.

Jon had been right about the tree being climbed. A full-size Soviet agent had carried the micro-saboteurs in a metal tank on his back and established them in the tree. He had bored a hole deep into the trunk and connected the tank to it by a tube.

He had climbed ten feet higher, topped the tree and bored two vertical holes in the stump. Into one he had dropped a fertile male and female termite, and into the other had inserted a half-inch-diameter steel tube with a dozen Soviet micro-engineers housed in its base.

Then he had left the tree.

Ten feet below the sawn-off treetop the main party of micro-engineers established a second breeding pair, exploding a charge at the end of the tunnel to create a bridal chamber for the royal couple who were carried into the interior of the tree from their cages in the transporter tank. They were to be the founders of the main termite colony. Both pairs mated and, while the two colonies grew, the engineers at the treetop started work on a lift shaft which would join the upper and lower territories. Far below, Russian micro-chemists injected a poisonous virus into the sap channels of the great pine.

As the tree died the termites proliferated.

When the inhabitants in the upper nest numbered several thousand, man performed an act of genocide on insect.

The Russians killed the queen and her king and slaughtered most of their progeny. They slit open the bellies of the dead creatures and spilled the contents on to the rough floors of the territory. The fluid dried as smooth and hard as marble and the engineers converted the passageways and breeding cells into laboratories and living quarters for the scientists. In the floor of the great, empty royal chamber they began the excavation of three shafts, using survivors from the butchered tribe as labourers.

In the depths of the tree the great dynamo of the lower territory gained momentum. Its galleries, its passages, its hatching cells, its nurseries, honeycombed the trunk and branches of the tree – eaten out by the voracious jaws of the queen's swarming offspring.

The original bridal chamber was now an arched hall, constantly enlarged to accommodate the growing volume of her majesty and her court. When the population reached a million and the dying tree was almost dried out, the shafts driven down from above carried water to the thirsty multitudes. The agent had sawn a V-shaped catchment area into the tree-stump and water flowed down it and filled the shafts. The burrows of the termites surrounded the bases of the shafts and water seeped through the thin walls into the territory.

Then the real work of the colony began.

The scientists ascended to their quarters at the top of the tree and started full-scale production of the virus.

This was the vital part of the Russian sabotage, understanding of which had eluded Dilke (though, from the cat-walk which led to the upper termitory, he had looked down on the brimming reservoir of green virus solution).

Central to the whole operation was the infection of the winged termites and their controlled release from the tree.

The contents of the virus well were piped to the bases of two branches and sprayed on to the departing insects. There they crowded the passageways which honeycombed the branches until – when wind and weather were right – the steel doors at the branch-tips were opened and the carriers of the tree disease were released into the night.

The defector had made an ample down-payment for political freedom! Now Dilke had information which would destroy the whole sabotage complex – if he could *escape* with it. He scowled at the embalmed bodies of protozoa in the glassy brown floor of his cell, then smiled wryly. His belief that he was cleverly cultivating Pavlov's friendship had been mistaken – the boot had been on the other foot!

A guard opened Dilke's cell door and Jonathan Butt dragged in two steel benches; Hyacinthe followed with bedding and the door was shut on them.

Whether Pavlov had caught the governor in a compliant mood or usurped his authority they never discovered, but they were together within twelve hours of Dilke's demand to speak to his companions.

The speed of the move left no doubt of Pavlov's anxiety to escape.

They were alone together for the first time since their capture.

Dilke leapt up and danced a silent jig of celebration – amazing them both with his sudden agility – then waltzed Hyacinthe round the narrow space between the bunks.

They halted and listened, staring breathlessly at each other until the guard moved away. They sat on the bunks, Hyacinthe took Dilke's left hand in both of hers and looked into his face.

'You are all right, Mathew!'

Dilke meshed his fingers with hers, smiled agreement and told them that he had kept up the pretence ever since his stay in the hospital.

He told them of his talk with Pavlov and of the Russian's reluctance to take part in an attack on the guards.

'And if the attempt fails *he'll* be in the clear!' exploded Butt. 'Can we trust him to go on with this, anyway?'

'I think so,' Dilke said.

'The man's a rabbit!'

'I think he'll be all right. He's tailor-made for defection: clever and industrious but unappreciated by his boss and his colleagues – even the engineers poke fun at him.'

Butt grunted acknowledgment and added, 'I think much of the research which Gravshenko takes the credit for is actually his assistant's.'

'Who looks forward to years of frustration as dogsbody to a vain old man.' Dilke paused and smiled grimly. 'I won't let him cool off. He has told me things I ought not to know. He is in too deep to draw back.'

They talked in low, animated voices; seated on the bunks with their heads almost touching; enjoying their freedom from surveillance and the end of their virtual isolation from each other.

Dilke told them of Pavlov's information about the virus incubation and its spread across the forests.

'I remember!' Hyacinthe exclaimed. 'The smell from the virus reservoir was the same as the termites which flew out of the tunnel.'

They talked about escape and were suddenly chilled by a realization of the risks involved. Rehearsal was impossible without knowledge of where and when the attempt would be made but they decided that if Pavlov failed to divert the attention of the guards Hyacinthe might do so with a pretence of fainting or hysteria.

Only Dilke was armed – he showed them the club-like bolt – and they examined the bunks, hoping to detach a metal strut for Jon, but they were welded solid. Butt recalled that his cell door now stood open. 'Maybe I could slip out the bolt when I pass the door and it would never be missed!' he scowled and slammed a huge fist into an open hand. 'If all else fails I have this!'

Twenty

Alexis Pavlov stood at the gateway to the lower territory with his eyes fixed on the second hand of his watch.

He wore a Geiger counter at his belt and held a clipboard under his arm. Perspiration beaded his cropped scalp and Dilke watched a dark stain of sweat grow between the shoulders of his blue tunic.

At noon he signalled to the gatekeeper and the steel door rumbled open, releasing a blast of stinking air.

Pavlov turned his head. The eyes which met Dilke's were glassy. Stiff with apprehension, the Russian nodded jerkily and Dilke gave a barely perceptible nod in reply.

They filed into the tunnel – a guard, Pavlov, Dilke, Hyacinthe, Butt, a second guard – and the door closed behind them. The light from the guards' rods glowed red on walls lacquered with termite excrement and a floor burnished by termite feet.

The air was hot, wet and foul. They stood and sweated while Pavlov adjusted the counter to one tick per second and scrawled a first reading on his notepad.

The lower territory was not wired for light but the check-points were marked by mounds of glow-worm eggs piled behind bars in deep alcoves.

The route which had been plotted went out to the eastern limits of the territory then back to the hatching and nursery areas. Their way through a maze of tunnels was marked by a luminous band – the fluid from glow-worm eggs—which stretched straight before them, deviating only to avoid dried-out sap channels like manholes in the floor. The air sighed in the tunnel. The hum from the heart of the nest—so insistent when they had first entered it—was fainter. The hot, moist breeze which had pressed on their backs was replaced by sweeter air which cooled their faces.

Ventilation.

Dilke suddenly remembered Gravshenko's old picture showing the Russian, the Negro and the spongelike concrete structure between them.

He recalled Gravshenko's demonstration of the movement of air within a territory; its entry through apertures in the outer walls and its circulation within.

Dilke wiped a sleeve across his sweating brow and thought about those apertures.

At Check-point Seven, green light shone through the bars. Suspended from the ceiling of the alcove was the pupa of a glow-worm, a living lantern in an advanced state of metamorphosis. From its tail cemented to the ceiling, to its head which almost touched the floor, the pupa was nine millimetres long. The final shape of the beetle was discernible through the casing which enclosed it; green light poured from its belly. Pavlov took a reading and moved on, but soon he stopped and Dilke could hear him arguing in a high, nervous voice with the front guard about Check-point Eight.

Was this the promised diversion?

Check-point Eight had disappeared. No glow-worm beacon shone in the tunnel ahead—only the eerie glow of the guideline.

There was an intersection ahead. The volume of sound from the Geiger counter increased. Just before the intersection Dilke saw a black hole in the wall of the tunnel and the glint of steel bars. Check-point Eight.

The bars were twisted and bent and the cage door was smashed. Something gleamed within the black hole – then suddenly moved.

A termite warrior crashed out of the broken cell and took Pavlov and the first guard in its huge pincered mandibles. The Russians were smashed together in a grotesque embrace within the closed ring of spiked jaws.

The great muscles inside the armoured head of the brute slowly tightened. Pavlov flailed at the chest and face of the guard and shrieked with pain and terror. The beast swung up its head, lifting the men from the floor; the jaws closed inexorably; there was a dull report as their lower vertebrae snapped and their bodies fell back from the waist. Pavlov's head and arms hung down, the inverted bow of his screaming mouth was a grin of agony; then his throat worked convulsively but no sound came out.

The second guard jumped forward. Dilke slid the bolt out of his shirt and clubbed him on the back of the skull. He swung the bolt with both hands and he hit very hard. The man fell on his face and his rod skittered along the floor.

The monster's jaws opened and the Russians fell out. Its great head swung from side to side and its jointed antennae whirled. There was something terrifying about the beast's lack of eyes. Dilke dragged Hyacinthe back. The beast's antennae vibrated, then pointed towards them, its jaws clashed together with extraordinary force – it took a tentative step forward.

They turned and ran down the tunnel and scrambled down a sap-hole in the floor. Iron-hard mandibles hit the edge of the hole. Dilke ducked his head and felt vibrations from the blow through the side of the shaft. The beast above them was like a mad thing, tramping around the hole and beating at its edge in a frenzy.

At last it moved away. Dilke cautiously raised his head to floor level – it stood motionless at the intersection of the tunnels. The fallen electric rods glowed on the floor with undiminished brilliance; Dilke sat on the edge of the hole and stared longingly at them. Slowly he hoisted himself up and knelt on the edge of the hole; the polished head of the warrior swung round.

The clubbed guard lay face down against the wall. The heel of his right boot jerked up, then fell again. Beyond him the bodies of Pavlov and the first guard shared a dreadful intimacy. The splintered bones of their pelvic cages were locked together and the Geiger counter rattled dully within the soft enclosure of their burst viscera.

The termite lowered its plated head and suddenly charged the wall. The sound of the blow thundered down the tunnel.

It stood and listened. Charged again and listened.

From far away came a faint answering thud.

Crash! Crash! Crash! The beast hammered furiously at the wall, grunting at each blow, wind whistling in its breathing tubes.

A staccato answer throbbed like a distant drum, followed by a pervasive hiss – the communal snarl which they had first heard in the queen's chamber.

The tunnel filled with termite alarm signals. A rapid fire of clicks and sonic whistles reverberated through the honeycomb of passages, returning again and again as a multiple echo to the ears of the fugitives. Through this wash of sound the insistent hammer blows of the warrior termite continued.

The first of the horde raced out of the darkness; a soldier ran without pause towards Dilke, who fell into the hole and scrambled down in panic, shouting to Hyacinthe and Butt to get further down the shaft.

The termite's body was too large to enter the sap-hole. It raged above them and raked the edge of the shaft with its scimitar mandibles, raining wood fragments down on their heads. A furious mob joined it, struggling around and across the hole. Above the uproar Dilke heard the Russian scream.

The shaft wall was rough, giving ample climbing holds.

They scrambled down into blackness.

In the dark, Dilke kicked Butt's head. They both swore. Hyacinthe's muffled voice came up from below.

'We've come to a stop!' fumed Butt.

Dilke straddled his legs and pushed with his feet and his back against the shaft walls. They were trapped in a pit, with a million giant bloody insects waiting for them at the top! Dilke's skin crawled.

'I'll go down and see,' Butt called.

Dilke heard the scuffle of two bodies passing each other in the narrow shaft; then there was silence.

The circle of red light above had so diminished that the gleaming limbs and bellies and jaws of the insects were indistinguishable. Dilke squinted down between his legs. Minutes passed; though he could not see his companions he thought he saw a faint blotch of light below. Then Butt called to Hyacinthe; Dilke heard the scrape of her boots, a gasp and a thud. The irregular patch of grey had become a circle of hardly discernible light; the way was now clear. Further down there were no more footholds – the shaft opened into a tunnel roof; he jammed himself into the end of the shaft and managed to reach down and find handholds, then swung awkwardly down.

Jonathan stood astride the saphole in the tunnel floor to prevent Dilke dropping into it; he took Dilke around the knees and lowered him.

From the shaft down which they had descended came the faint continuing sounds of termite fury.

Dilke faced into the air which flowed along the tunnel.

What light there was came from behind him, from the heart of the territory. The ventilation passage through which air from the outer world came was pitch black, and out of the blackness throbbed alarm signals from warriors guarding the ventilation openings. The rods which would have armed them and lighted their way were in the tunnel high above, glowing uselessly near the dead bodies of the Russians.

Sweat started out on Dilke's face and cropped head then dried in the cold air.

They had found an escape route – but he realized bitterly that they could not use it.

The attempt at escape had failed.

Pavlov had got his freedom!

They would be lucky if they escaped with their lives.

They had to go back. He turned wearily towards the light and led the way.

The light by which they travelled was infinitely soft, filtering down through a network of tunnels. Dimly reflected from irregularities in the polished walls and floors. Visible only because their sight had sharpened remarkably during their climb down the unlit shaft.

They travelled slowly west, feeling their way along the darker stretches; guided by the current of fresh air behind them. As they moved deeper into the tree the temperature rose and the airflow became variable. They wandered without direction, backtracking, stopping for whispered discussions, retreating from the sound of marching termite feet.

But always they moved higher towards the upper passageways and the light grew stronger.

At last they found the glow-worm track.

The discordant sounds of alarm had ceased, replaced by the steady hum of termite industry; but as they hurried along the glowing path they saw more and more termites flitting palely across tunnel intersections – and they walked in fear of discovery.

A young termite at an intersection ahead of them begged food from passing workers. The fugitives waited tensely for it to go, but it had established a little territory of its own, a base from which to do its begging and from which it strayed only a few paces. When Dilke muttered and impatiently shifted his feet the termite ran towards them. It was an infant just out of its first moult, plump and moist, the white fat of its body shining through its translucent skin. It was waist high and raised its head to them like a sucking calf. Hyacinthe gave a strangled squeak and they waited in horror for it to cry out in alarm. But it placidly explored their legs and bodies with trembling antennae then loitered away; they jogged past it.

Danger increased as they approached the place of escape. They saw more and more termites, and several times they huddled down in silence when packs of soldiers crossed their path.

At last they turned a corner and the gate was before them.

They staggered forward, numb with strain and fatigue.

In dread of a last-minute attack, Dilke kicked and pounded on the heavy gate.

A red light immediately flashed on. The gate clanged open. They stood blinded by the glare and hands reached out and pulled them forward. After the repulsive termite tunnels the grimy white corridor seemed clinical, the hard-faced Russians as welcome as old friends.

Dilke and his companions slumped down with legs stretched out and their backs to the wall and concentrated on breathing.

Foreman Listnitsky stood in the doorway and stared into the territory before interrogating Dilke in mangled English.

Dilke breathlessly described the ambush at Checkpoint Eight and explained how Pavlov and the guards had been killed by the lurking termite warrior. And how he and his companions had escaped – he wiped the blood from a graze on his cheek, got when scrambling down the sap-hole – and what experiences they'd endured.

At Listnitsky's invitation he retold the ambush bit – in detail and without variation.

Kubric arrived during the third repetition and took the foreman aside. Listnitsky understood English better than he spoke it; his account – in Russian – of Dilke's story was faultless.

Kubric stayed only a minute.

He nodded at the open gate. 'Shut that!' His eyes passed coldly over the sprawling survivors. 'Take them away. Separate them and lock them up.'

He walked stiffly down the corridor.

Twenty-one

The bulb had been removed from Dilke's cell, either as a measure of economy or as part of a new hard-line policy by his gaolers.

He was alone again and the blackness of his cell matched his mood. He had passed sleepless hours recalling the failure of the attempted escape and remembering the expression in Kubric's pale eyes as he heard Dilke's version of the attack on the patrol.

Dilke sat tensely on the edge of his bunk, aware of unusual activity in the passageways outside. Deprived of vision his ears seemed to have become more sensitive – hearing faint calls and shouted answers … the sound of many footsteps along the main corridor, moving towards the distant lift shaft … the throb of the lift engine …

He heard a strange sound: a droning vibration, sensitive to touch rather than hearing. He hunted for the tumbler in his mattress and put it to the wall.

Through the glass the vibrations became a doleful sequence of seven notes; mournful as the song of seals or a warning of fog. Six semitones rising to a long-drawn minor C. Repeated every ten seconds.

The effect was soporific. Dilke leaned with closed eyes against the wall of his black cell. He became aware of Russian voices in the pauses between the seven-tone sequence. They spoke quietly and in monosyllables, their sentences fragmented by the signal; but enough came through for Dilke to understand that they were discussing the radio equipment: only tapes of weather bulletins and logging-camp talk were to be taken – the heavy stuff was to be left behind.

He heard a door crash open. A third voice shouted above the dirge of the radio signal, 'Switch that thing off, Sorokin!'

It was Gravshenko, his voice hoarse with anger.

'What are you doing, Kubric? I decide when the recall signal shall go out! The labs are empty! Where are the men? I will ... I will ... ' His voice choked hysterically.

There was a click, a pause, then Kubric's voice filled the silence.

'All the men are down at their assembly stations in the transporter tank. Everyone must be strapped in by twelve. We have taken your files but not your laboratory equipment.'

'Who are you speaking to? Are you speaking to me, Kubric?' Gravshenko shrilled. 'You are speaking to the governor. By what right have you ordered these things? My work is not finished ... '

Kubric's voice interrupted venomously. 'Your work is sabotage – not research – and was completed last autumn. I have taken control, Gravshenko. My report will say why. No doubt the Committee of Civil Disruption and Economic Sabotage will be interested in your *research*. And in the fact that we are now down to ten days' supply of fuel. And that we should have left here six months ago and that I have lost forty men in that time ... '

'The engineers are *your* responsibility,' shouted the governor, 'they're not my concern! I will *break* you, Kubric!'

Dilke heard Gravshenko leave at a shambling run.

The door slammed and the muffled steps faded.

'How long will this tape run, Sorokin?' Kubric said sharply.

'For six hours, Comrade Kubric, but if I set it on repeat it will run until the power is cut.'

'Set it on repeat, then lock the door and get to your couch.'

Twenty-two

Dilke's cell door was opened and he stumbled out with his eyes screwed up against the light.

Kubric stood alone in the passage armed with a rod. He unlocked the next door and Butt emerged, blinking.

The Russian put his back against the third door and signalled the way they must go, but Dilke hesitated, waiting for the release of Hyacinthe.

'Hurry.' It was the first English word Kubric had used. He accompanied it with a decisive swing of the rod.

They went reluctantly into the main corridor and out to the cat-walk that crossed the great hall; their thoughts, dark with premonition, whirling around the fact of the girl's absence.

They had crossed three reservoirs and reached Shaft Four when Jonathan Butt's footsteps slowed almost to a stop. 'Mathew!' he hissed, 'I don't like this!'

There was an explosive shout.

A jolting shock seared the palm with which Dilke touched the cat-walk rail. He spun round.

Jonathan Butt stood with his legs spread wide, clutching the rails with both fists, glaring at a point above Dilke's head. His massive body arched backwards, revealing the thick, veined throat below the tangled beard. His legs slowly gave way and he fell to his knees with a crash, his glazed eyes fixed on Dilke's chest, his bottom lip hung loose.

Kubric stood behind him and brought down the blazing rod again. It was like a benediction. The expression on Kubric's smooth white face was remote, almost melancholy, and the slow movement of his descending hand seemed almost gentle.

There was a firecracker explosion when the tip of the rod touched the crown of the kneeling man's head, and the hair stood out from his scalp porcupine-stiff. Butt's eyes blazed, his teeth snapped together in a snarl and he jerked in the top rails of the cat-walk as if they were made of tallow.

It was the convulsion of death. One hand remained hooked to a sagging rail, the other relinquished its hold and the body fell loosely forward, swung across the walk and lay half over its edge. A drift of smoke rose from the cleft scalp.

Kubric knocked the great fist loose with the heavy base of his weapon, kicked at a sprawling leg, and the body slipped off the cat-walk on to the chute. It slid down the incline, greased by the passage of a thousand dead termites, gathered momentum and shot through the narrow hole.

Visible through the hole were slopes covered by dead, white trees; dazzling bright in the mid-morning sun.

Dilke's gaze was frozen on the point where the body had disappeared into space, then he sprinted to the door at the end of the cat-walk.

He knocked back the bolt and dragged the door open. It moved with an awful, ponderous slowness. He looked back wildly; Kubric stood with the rod on his shoulder, a hand resting on the cat-walk rail.

Dilke squeezed past the half-open door into the unlit passageway. A rank smell of insects filled the

G   193

air and a faint, sibilant sound came from the dark interior.

Dilke shuddered. Slowly the ghostly forms of termites crowding the passage became discernible. The pale beasts turned their heads towards him and shifted restlessly away from the light – but an angry soldier pushed forward, hissing with rage.

Dilke recoiled in horror, leapt through the doorway and shoved at the door with all his strength.

The soldier burst through the crowd of workers and charged.

The door closed, the bolt slammed home with a crash. Dilke heard the clang of the termite's armoured head as it hit the door then the exploratory scrape of its mandibles. He lay back against the cold steel, gasping.

Kubric had not moved. His thin lips parted fractionally to reveal neat white teeth, then he moved forward without haste.

There was no escape. All the force of Dilke's mind and body – channelled before into animal panic and attempted flight – now powered a blazing rage, an ecstasy of fury which destroyed his fear of the weapon which Kubric carried.

Butt was dead. Only the death of his killer would discharge the shaking tension which possessed Dilke. He crouched and stepped towards the Russian. Then he saw an abandoned rod hooked over the cat-walk rail. He strode forward, grabbed the weapon and zipped it up to Kill. The tip did not light; the battery was dead. Dilke grinned with rage and danced forward with the rod outstretched.

Kubric halted. His eyes were contemptuous, he raised his blazing weapon, took a short quick step forward and thrust at Dilke's body. Dilke parried the thrust. Kubric lunged again. Dilke parried – the rod glanced off and its heat scorched his shoulder. Kubric stepped away, grunted, then hit savagely at Dilke's head. Dilke swung two-handed at the approaching rod. Kubric's weapon was struck from his hand, there was a thud and a hiss as it hit the wall of Shaft Four and was quenched in the slurry at the bottom.

Kubric ran with a curious lack of dignity. Till now Dilke had seen him move always with deliberation; the act of running revealed that his body was abnormally long, supported on short, thick legs. He ran clumsily but with great vigour and rapidity, pounding furiously along the metal walk. Dilke could not gain on him. The Russian fled into the corridor and headed for the lift shaft. He turned at top speed into the cul-de-sac, bounced off the wall, hurled himself down the passage and through the open lift door.

As the door slammed shut Dilke threw the rod like a javelin from ten paces away. The heavy block of batteries hit the porthole and flew off into the water which boiled around the lift.

Dilke stood panting at the water's edge and watched the lift go down shuddering, its propeller threshing at full power.

Kubric's face appeared at the round window. The glass had splintered but not broken. His waxen features were dislocated by the fan of cracks; below the displaced eyes his small and even teeth were bared in a grimace of hatred, or derision.

Porthole and face disappeared below the surface. Dilke swore with an excess of violence and glared down at the receding light, shaken into luminous fragments by the turbulent water.

Then he gave a yell, smashed his fist against the wall and raced away through the corridors leading to the cells. Wrenching the heavy bolt from his cell door he ran into the store-room, broke open a case and, clutching half a dozen grenades to his chest, sprinted back to the lift shaft.

He pulled the pin from a grenade and tossed it into the black circle of water. It went down fast, the handle spinning behind its heavy head. He sent the rest after it.

The first explosion was deep and dull, then a chain of detonations became one long boom.

The floor shook. A lace of white spume sped up from below, a solid column of water hit the ceiling and broke into foam. Dilke was swept down the passage and hurled against a wall. He coughed up water and staggered back to the shaft. No flotsam from the lift had surfaced – in fact the water level was far below, almost out of sight, sinking fast. A stream of cold air followed the sinking water; there was a deep subterranean hiccup and then silence.

Dilke sat down at the side of the shaft and stared at the rills of water which streamed into the empty black pit.

He touched a cut on his lip with his tongue, wiped blood from his chin, then returned to the cells and freed Hyacinthe.

They clung together in silence. At last she said, 'You're bleeding, Mathew!' Then, 'Where's Jon?'

'I want your help,' Dilke answered. They carried the case of grenades between them and staggered up on to the cat-walk over the reservoirs. There were eighteen grenades left; he laid them in neat rows on the walk above the shafts — six for each shaft — moved quickly from point to point and methodically flighted them into the water at intervals of one second; then ran to crouch beside Hyacinthe in the shelter of the corridor.

Within the confined space the noise of the explosions was shattering. Their eyes shut tight involuntarily and they pressed their palms against their ears.

Far below, water flooded the lower levels of the termitory.

Dilke had a vision of tumbling, swirling water and a drowning queen. Of water-filled corridors and dormitories and workshops. Of water pouring through the tunnel which linked tree to tank then cascading into its hold. He saw a nightmare of wide eyes and screaming mouths. Choking men writhing in the harness which bound them to their couches. Breath gushing from their throats and bubbling to the surface of the rising water.

Dilke opened his eyes and shuddered.

They rose, dazed by the shock waves, and walked to the end of the corridor and stared into the cavern. Subsiding waters still boomed in the ruptured shafts. The explosions of water had wrecked the cat-walk and also put out the lights. Only ice-blue daylight, shining through the disposal chute and gleaming on walls running with water, illuminated the cave.

This time they could make it.

The distant ray of cold light marked their way to the outside world.

Hyacinthe asked again for Butt.

'Jon is dead, my love,' Dilke said, and pulled her to him.

She cried silently, gave a single sob then pushed away from him. 'I *hate* them,' she said bitterly.

They descended and scrambled along ridges between shallow lakes on the uneven floor of the cave. The sour smell of the virus solution filled the air and its spores were like seaweed beneath their feet.

At last they came to Shaft Four. The frame which supported the cat-walk was still intact; they climbed its criss-crossed girders and crawled on to the metal path. Below them five termites paddled weakly around the flooded shaft with pearls of oxygen floating from their breathing tubes. Dilke felt no pity — only disgust.

He winched down the cable from above the shaft, secured it to a rail and dropped the end down the chute. They went down hand over hand, slipping and sliding on the metal surface towards the light.

PART FIVE

Twenty-three

Mountains. Hills. Valleys. Trees. A river.

World without end. Sky everlasting.

They lay together on a ledge below the chute.

A flaring orb danced in space above the mountains and Dilke closed his eyes against its brilliance.

The source of all light and warmth – of all life – suffused their skins. Its radiance entered their bodies and turned their flesh to gold; it touched their brows, penetrated the thin membranes of their eyelids and filled their heads with soft light, veiling their dark memories of confinement and death. The passing time stood still. They floated voluptuously in an infinity of silence and felt a liberation of the spirit too profound for laughter or tears.

The air was cooler and the sun lay far to the west.

Dilke listened to the quiet noises of his own body; a singing in his ears and the pulse of blood in his throat.

He turned his head and looked at Hyacinthe for a long minute. She lay with her eyes closed and her lips parted moistly as if in drugged sleep. Soon they must go. He reached out and gently ran the side of a finger down her black cheek.

She opened her eyes and rather sadly returned his smile.

'We must move on, Hyacinthe. Until we reach our top camp we won't eat. If we climb till dark we should reach the camp tomorrow.'

He crawled to the edge of the ledge and peered down. The tent roof was a spot of green on the topmost branch; it would be a full day's climb down to it. He leaned farther out; an infinitely greater distance below a tiny spot of yellow marked the matchbox.

A scatter of sound came from the south. They searched the sky and found a silvered dot which grew in size and clattered in the air above them.

The helicopter hung for a moment before spiralling down to the riverbank. Its motor back-fired, then was silent and the great vanes free-wheeled to a stop.

Dilke's face was bitter. They had escaped too late. He had believed they had ample time to reach Brymay. He waited for Bellamy's clumsy descent from the machine, but only the pilot got out.

The man removed his wool jacket, took a rattling bundle of metal and leather equipment from the cab and set off up the slope towards their tree.

Dilke lay prone on the ledge eighty feet up and watched the man. He sat on a tree root and smoked as he sorted out the equipment; then he put on harness and buckled the metal spikes to his boots.

Understanding slowly came to Dilke.

The man stood up, dropped his cigarette and kicked it out, then took a long leather strap in his right hand. With a swing of his arm he sent the strap around the tree, catching the end in his left hand. Then he buckled it, enclosing himself and the trunk in a leather loop. He leaned back against the strap, kicked the spikes in and began to climb. He climbed slowly and easily, patiently negotiating branches, halting to rest occasionally and watch the setting sun.

As the sun went down shadow filled the river valley, moved up the rocky slope, reached the base of the pine and followed the climber in slow pursuit.

The thud and slap of the climber's ascent grew louder and, near the treetop, Hyacinthe and Dilke were jolted with increasing violence.

At last he reached the branch which supported the metal tank and sat astride the branch. He paused for breath; then, taking the tank in both hands he pulled gently. The tank did not move, he pulled harder and it came loose.

A stream of liquid poured from the tube which had attached tank to tree. The climber sat and stared; the flow became a trickle.

Then the man screamed.

He scrambled to his feet and the tank fell off the branch.

A cloud of winged insects rose like smoke from the holes which he had spiked in the brittle surface of the branch.

His enormous head was level with the ledge where Dilke and Hyacinthe crouched in fear and astonishment.

A force-ten scream came from Jacques Genet's cavernous throat. The black forest of his moustache bristled above monolithic teeth.

He scrabbled at his legs with one hand and clutched the tree with the other.

Warrior termites tumbled out of the branch amongst the swarming flyers. A score of them clung to him, their mandibles piercing and meeting in his flesh. Blotches, like splashes of crimson rain, appeared on his cord breeches. He plucked frantically at the brutes with blood-slippery fingers, tearing away the pale bodies, but the black, armoured heads remained anchored in the gashed flesh.

His huge eyes, bulging with pain and terror, rolled down to stare at the nightmare things swarming on his legs. A torrent of French came from his screaming mouth.

He scrambled back clumsily, smashing more holes in the shaking branch.

He squealed, flailed with his hands at his crutch and danced off the branch into space.

He fell like a sky-diver with spread arms and legs, coloured red by the setting sun, then vanished into the black shadow which had followed him up the tree.

Defenders of a monarchy which had lost its queen, saved by their presence in galleries which had escaped flooding, the warriors retreated to the holes from which they had emerged.

High above them the two tiny humans watched them swing their menacing heads and heard the distant whistle of their alarm calls to workers who hurried to repair the holes in the damaged branch.

Twenty-four

The moonlit pine towered above the surrounding dead trees. Within its tall white column lay the extinct source of the forest's destruction. A black cancerous labyrinth, foul and moist and corrupt like a great diseased lung which would breathe no more pestilence into the night air.

Hyacinthe and Mathew Dilke slept on a ledge near the treetop. Dilke woke from a dream of drowned men lying in numbered caskets. Pale, calm faces gleaming in dark water. Kazakov, Petronovitch, Gravshenko …

It was cold.

As soon as they reached Brymay he would contact Bellamy through Vancouver. There were many Jacques Genets in the world, for Russia was never short of agents, but there was no future for sabotage in the forests of the West now.

It was *very* cold. He huddled nearer to the sleeping girl and examined the stars.